J. F. DANSKIN

The Broken Circle

The Druid Stones Saga Book 1

Contents

Samhain

It was Samhain. This year, the same as every year, the people of Cardhu were to have a great celebration to mark the end of harvest, and the beginning of winter.

It was bright after many days of rain, and sun was gradually sliding towards the horizon – the sea, the islands – lands that had long been lost by the kingdom to the strangers in their longships. Donnell stood close to the Celtic Rock, nursing a tankard full of mead. With no family of his own, he was known to all but close to few. He certainly didn't want to celebrate with the farmer Tarin and his kin, on whose lands he had been forced to work now for many years.

Nearby, some children were playing at raiding, fighting with sticks; others pretended to be druids, or even wulvers and hags. One boy – or rather, a young man almost grown and nearing his bonding time – was holding a pretend shield as well as a wooden spear. He shouted, "the boggles are attacking from the forest!" and then began to run off towards the nearby roundhouses. And a group of children of all ages, mostly younger, ran after him.

Many of the adults were sitting around the village square, some of them having already consumed more mead than was wise. A few had already retired to their roundhouses to sleep or drink more into the night, despite the early hour.

Donnell narrowed his eyes slightly, uncomfortable with the careless behaviour that some villagers were exhibiting – were there not enough threats abroad that people knew to be wary? Besides, the Samhain ceremony proper had not even begun. Too few, in Donnell's view, waited by the Rock to watch the druids renew their protective enchantments, the way he had been taught to do when his mother was still alive. It made no difference to the enchantments whether they were observed or not, but at least, Donnell thought, they should show enough respect to wait and watch in silence.

But then as he looked around, his frown softened. Down the slope towards the centre of the village, his childhood friend Malcolm was approaching, a man of twenty-three summers who looked somewhat older due to his thinning hair and mighty dark beard. Donnell continued to stand by the Rock and smiled as he caught his friend's eye. Malcolm, spotting him, hurried over.

"Well met," said Donnell, raising his drink and grinning. "For a while, I thought that nobody else was coming to the festivities. Someone needs to keep the ways of Samhain."

But Malcolm did not seem to be in a festive mood. "Have you heard?" he said. "Norse longships have been sighted. I just came from Weir."

"You've spend the day with the fisherfolk?" asked Donnell. He was surprised, for Samhain was a great celebration among their village, and everybody did their best to spend it at home. He peered westwards towards the shore, standing on tiptoes. It was an uphill walk of over half an hour from the sea's edge, and there had to be a good reason for Malcolm to return so late in the day.

"Well, yes. I have just left Alna's clan gathering. But I wanted to see you all before the day was out."

Alna was a woman from among the village people of Weir – the nearest settlement on the shore to Cardhu itself. The people there were mostly unrelated to the Cardhu villagers, and they also lived a very different way, fishing and selling their wares rather than working the land. They were a close-knit and at times unfriendly people, who did not partake in the old ceremonies, instead worshipping what Donnell thought of as the Irish religion. Donnell knew that his friend was keen to start courting the woman. If they were to marry, she would have to renounce her family's ways and come to Cardhu, he supposed.

Donnell rested a hand on the man's shoulder. "Well, then – take a swig of mead, and tell me what you saw."

Nodding slightly, Malcolm complied, reaching across with his right hand. The former apprentice blacksmith had suffered the loss of his lower left arm in an accident in his father's forge when they were just youngsters, but could manage almost any task one handed, including wielding a weapon. He drained half of the mug, and then handed it back to Donnell.

"Not I. The folk down at Weir. They say the Norse ships have been active up the coast. They were sighted near Inverkip several times over the past day, and by Wherrycross, too."

"Well… but that needn't mean much," said Donnell. "Just seeing them in their ships. They could be trading, perhaps?"

"Perhaps. But her people really don't think so. This is different from usual. The Norse have landed to the north of here, and have been examining some ruins and ancient foundations. According to Alna's cousin, that only happens when they plan to build. Some of the clan believe that they will established what they call a long-fort, and overwinter on this coast."

"All right…"

"And that usually means an invasion is coming. So her cousin says, anyhow, and his own people were forced from their lands before he came to Weir."

Donnell put one hand on Malcolm's shoulder again. "My friend, it doesn't sound like they are bringing war tonight. So relax and enjoy yourself – it's Samhain. The people of Weir might not respect the ways of the Old North, but we at least can show a bit of gratitude to the gods. They are, after all, our protectors."

"But the Norse…"

"Norsemen have been over on the islands with their ships, and troubling the north coast for years, and they have never shown any interest in attacking Ystrad Clud. And if they did spend the winter on these shores, it needn't mean that they would do anything to harm us. If they tried, the druids would help us. Their power would protect the kingdom."

"That's true. I just…" Malcolm's mouth opened and closed again as he looked towards the shore, and then he turned back to his friend. "Well, all right then. never mind."

There was shouting in the distance, and Donnell's heart skipped a beat; he looked around to see if Norsemen and their longships truly had come to harry the people of Cardhu. But it was a happier sight that met his eyes. All along the main track through the village, people were emerging from their houses and shouting in delight at the coming of five cloaked figures with their hoods thrown back, marching slowly in his direction.

The druids had arrived.

* * *

In the dwindling light, the festival proceeded much as it had done every year that Donnell could remember. The five druids stood around the Celtic Rock in a circle, not touching, for the rock was the size of a small fishing vessel, and even if they had stretched out their arms while around it, their hands would not have met.

Together the druids were considered the greatest of their kind, the Mor-druids, each wiser and more magical than the travelling storytellers or local healers who were also sometimes referred to as druids. Each one of the five represented a clan, and had powers and responsibilities passed on from parent to child. Each druid was holding a staff or wand, and was wearing a drab and patched woollen cloak, and most had long hair tied back, but for one – a woman with flaming red curly hair that hung loose. Donnell knew her to be the healer, Fenella.

After touching the Rock, the druids then slowly walked over to the mysterious ring-shaped markings in the ground nearby. Each took it in turns to put their staff into a single indentation that had filled up with rainwater, and then spoke his or her own prayer to their preferred god. For each of the five had an affinity with one of the gods who watched over the people of Ystrad Clud. Fenella, Donnell knew, represented Brighid, the goddess of healing and fire, while a tall grey-haired druid by the name of Congal favoured Lugh, the great crafter and leader of the gods. This appeared to make Congal the leader of the druids, too. The allegiances of the others he was less sure of.

As he looked around the group, he realised that one of the druids looked unfamiliar. Between Fenella and Congal stood a short, sharp-faced woman with a newer and darker-coloured cloak than the others. She carried a staff, but it was plain, and unadorned, unlike the others which were intricately carved.

Donnell's eyes flicked from side to side, taking in the other faces of the druids. He had expected to see someone different – Gabrán, a dark-haired druid who typically carried no staff, but instead a long wooden wand. What had happened to him?

Today, for sure, there were only two men in the gathering, that was for sure. He glanced around at Malcolm, but his friend was barely paying attention…

* * *

"I was wondering what happened to your companion," said Donnell to the two cloaked figures.

With the ceremony over, he was taking the farmer's three horses from the outfield back to the stable where they spent the night – as did Donnell, as he lived in a small room at the back of the stable. It might be Samhain, the end of the harvest, but some farming work still needed to be done.

The tall druid, Congal – the man he had always assumed to be their leader – looked around as Donnell spoke. "These are fine beasts," said Congal. "Are they yours?" The other druid also looked around – the flame-haired Fenella, the healer.

"No. These belong to one of the farmers," said Donnell. "I just look after them."

"Are you not still a woodsman?" asked Fenella.

Donnell nodded slightly, feeling grateful that the mighty druids had deigned to pay enough attention to know even this information. "I trained with Macswain at the Laird's castle and lands. But for six summers I have been working Tarin's land, helping with the animals in exchange for food and board, and to repay my family's debt." He patted Beira, the great chestnut mare who was the strongest of the three horses, and added, "It's all right. I like animals."

They looked at each other in silence for a moment, and Donnell was on the verge of moving on without a response to his initial question, when Congal spoke again: "Our fellow druid – Gabrán – had to take a trip, and has been delayed. We look forward to welcoming him back very soon."

"I hope he returns safely, then. There have been longships sighted on the water."

Nodding his farewell to the venerable druids, Donnell walked away from them, and continued down the track to the stable. After settling the animals and seeing to their food and water, he walked back out. It was now almost entirely dark, but the sky was clear, and the lingering fingers of sunset in the west still provided enough light to see by as he walked out to the edge of the village. Walking out by himself held more appeal than the revelry in the village; he was tired, and would have to rise early, too.

Ahead, a set of low outcropping cliffs, a bluff, provided a viewpoint over the sea and sky beyond. It was a popular place for children to play; as a child, he had often climbed the rocks with Malcolm and others of his age, daring each other to stand far out at the edge. It was a beautiful spot, and commanded a view of the whole village of Cardhu to his left, and the string of coastal settlements could also be seen. His eyes narrowed for a moment as he looked towards the mouth of the river – the place of the new Norse long-fort, according to Malcolm. After a moment, he shrugged. In this light, he thought, there could be an army of Norsemen camped there and he wouldn't know any better.

Settling himself on the nearest part of the bluff, a large shelf of granite that stuck directly out over the fields below, Donnell looked again at the nearby coast and saw an old man with a short white beard making his way along the Laird's road near the small fishing settlement of Weir. He couldn't make out well from here in the dim light, but it looked very like the old man Eochaid – a mysterious figure who was said to be a lore master and a spellcaster, and who had informally tutored Donnell and Malcolm during their childhood. But they hadn't seen him for years. Could it really be him? Was he abroad, and if so, what was he doing down at Weir, on the night of Samhain?

The Message

Months passed, through the cold season and the rains, until springtime arrived.

Donnell was running his usual errands for the farmer Tarin when he noticed that something was happening in the centre of Cardhu – a visitor had arrived. A small crowd of villagers had gathered in their usual way, pretending to do something else, and getting within earshot without appearing to come too close.

He passed Niamh, a crofter who lived in a tiny roundhouse in front of one of the infields nearby. Her husband Cillian had died two years before, but she was a strong and capable woman, relied upon by many of the locals for her wisdom. She also had two half-grown children and a toddler to raise, though, and she currently held the small child by one hand, and a heavy-looking food sack in the other.

"What news?" Donnell asked.

"A visitor has arrived from Wherrycross," she answered. "Carrying a message from the Laird, they are saying, though I'd need to hear it myself before I could be sure of that." She slightly raised the sack that she was carrying. "Do you need any turnips?"

"Thanks," he smiled, "I may well do. Tarin is careless about horse feed – we are always running low – but it's not easy to get a silver groat out of him to buy supplies. I'll come back to you about that after I've picked up oats from Wallace. That's where I'm going now."

Donnell continued on his way to the main square, passing the Celtic Rock as he went. As he looked around, he noticed that several of the cup-shaped markings below the Rock had filled up with dirt and earth – they could easily be covered completely by the time the druids next visited in a few months time. That would look careless. Ungrateful. He stooped for a moment and began to clear one out with his hand, only to realise that it would take too long. He would have to come back to it.

He continued on to the street that ran through the main cluster of roundhouses of the village, and sighed when he spotted Ogledd. The man was the Laird's Luftenand in the village, and therefore ruler over Donnell and all of the other villagers of Cardhu. He styled himself as a warrior, but Donnell had known him since their childhood; back then, Ogledd had been cowardly and weak, but also the most arrogant and cruel of children. Nothing had changed. Donnell was generally pleased to see as little as possible of the man, and indeed Ogledd had not been seen much of late, as he had been entertaining several of his distant clansmen on his farm at the far northern edge of the village.

Ogledd was dressed in his finest clothes, an elaborate outfit of dyed blue and orange wool that he obviously thought lent him an air of nobility, and certainly made him stand out from the drab colours of most of the villagers all around. He was speaking to a woman who Donnell recognised as Macswain, the Laird's chief hunter. The Laird lived in the nearby town of Wherrycross, to the south, and Macswain was rarely seen in the surrounding villages. Short, muscular and dressed in simple hunting clothes, her appearance contrasted strikingly with the tall and flamboyant Ogledd.

"Here he is," said Macswain, spotting Donnell as he approached, and giving him a curt wave to come over.

Ogledd glanced round, and looked down his nose at Donnell. After a pause, he said, "Oh, yes, you are right. I think that is him."

Donnell snorted at the pretence of unfamiliarity, but walked closer to the man. "I have to collect feed for Tarin's horses, so this had better be quick," he said.

"We'll only take a minute of your time," said Ogledd, still attempting to look down at Donnell, despite their similarity in terms of height. "And then after that, perhaps another three or four days." He laughed to himself in a high-pitched voice.

Macswain didn't laugh or smile, but nodded slightly at Donnell. The woman was twenty years his elder, and one of the few people who could navigate through the local forests and moors better than he could, as he knew well – she had trained him in forest craft when he was just a youth. He ignored the Laird's Luftenand, and looked at his former mentor. "What's this about?" he asked.

"The Laird is expecting a visit, a grand gathering of his royal clan," she said. "We need you to take a message to his brother Tudorr ab Owain, at his broch up at Inverkip."

"Why me, Macswain? I have duties here. The crofters are getting their lands prepared for planting at this time of year, and Tarin need me to work the horses in his fields."

"But this is a matter of importance," said Macswain, her eyes narrowing slightly at the response. "We need someone who can travel quickly there and back with a response, and Luftenand Ogledd here recommended you – and I have to say, I agree. The quickest way will involve cutting through Holm's Wood, and I imagine you are better than anyone else in the village at travelling through the forest, not to mention by far the best with a spear or a bow." She briefly glanced around. "Unless Branwen has returned to Cardhu…?"

"No, she hasn't," Donnell replied shortly. "Anyway, as I say, I am needed elsewhere. It was good to see you, Macswain, but now I really need to be getting on."

He began to walk, but Macswain put a hand on his shoulder. "Donnell. I am afraid this is not a request."

Donnell took a deep breath, cursing inwardly. He loved to travel out across the surrounding lands – especially through forest, of course – but this trip would take two days there and two days back, possibly longer, even riding on Beira's back. There was work to do, and Tarin couldn't be trusted to take care of the animals at the best of times. They were now deep into springtime, and he feared that in his absence, the farmer would bring in someone inexperienced to help, which might lead to the other horses being overworked and harmed.

"The task simply *must* be done," added Macswain. "The Laird wills it."

He pursed his lips then nodded once. "And the fee?" he asked.

"Come," she said simply, leading him away from the other villagers who had drawn closer as they spoke. "Your time would be paid, of course. Five silver groats now, and another ten on your return, provided that the message reaches its destination in good time."

Donnell thought for a moment. It was true that such money would make a real difference to him. "Well, Macswain…"

"But there's more," she said, interrupting with a note of excitement in her voice as she looked her former apprentice directly in the eye. "The Laird is willing to free you from your bond to the farmer, too."

"What?" Donnell could barely believe what he was hearing. After all of these years of work to settle his family debt, the Laird could simply tell Tarin to release him?

"Would that help matters?" Macswain prompted.

"Without doubt," he replied slowly. "I would jump at the chance, of course, if I was at liberty to do so. But I don't think that Tarin will let me away from my duties on the farm even just to make this journey, unfortunately. He can't manage without my work with the horses, and there are crops to plant."

She put her hands on her hips and narrowed her eyes. "The fields can wait for a couple of days, Donnell."

He paused. A part of him was already running through the route north in his head, imagining the feeling of the wind in his hair, the slight sense of danger. It had been too long. And the prospect of an early relase from his bonded servitude to the farmer…Well, that would mean *freedom*. He could resume the forest work which suited him so much better, and perhaps even establish a home and family of his own.

"I'll find a way to make it happen," he said at last, with a firm nod. "Thank you. But I *will* need to go and collect the supplies." He pointed downhill towards the shore, where Wallace's farm was located. "I can't ride out for this length of time without leaving feed for the animals."

She nodded, and counted out five silver coins, which he tucked into the pouch on his belt.

"So, where is this message?"

"Ogledd has it. Collect it from him."

"So be it. I will do so on my return. Well met, Macswain. See you on the forest trails."

And without a word to Ogledd, Donnell turned and hurried away.

* * *

He had spoken again to Niamh and parted with one of the silver coins in exchange for her delivering the sack of turnips to the stable, as well as asking her eldest daughter to check on the horses in his absence. It was not his duty to pay for animal feed, but he wanted to do what he could to ensure that the beasts would be fed.

Now, cutting left from the road, Donnell walked down a path that was sometimes used as a shortcut towards Wherrycross, at least by those on foot; the trail ahead was rutted and full of potholes, though passable provided that a walker's boots were sufficiently sturdy, and their legs too.

The morning was bright and clear. He should set out northwards as early as possible, he thought, as the weather could change rapidly at this time of year. He looked out over the sea, and to the cluster of islands beyond where the Norsemen ruled the land, and their own folk never ventured – Cumbrae, Bute, Arran, the latter with some specks of snow still visible towards its peaks. Some boats and small ships could be seen, just dots from this distance, but all looked calm.

The path wound gradually down, through the remnants of old groundwork defences which were now just mounds of grass with some tumbledown walls and trees growing tall on both sides. After some time, Donnell reached a field used only by one of the outlying farmers – Robert Wallace's sheep farm, the second largest patch of land in Cardhu. From here he knew he could cut across to the main shore road a few hundred paces on, but Donnell instead followed the line of drystone walls that enclosed the herd.

Before long he was knocking at the door in the centre of the long, low, stone-built house. Wallace's residence was unlike the roundhouses up in Cardhu, although it was usually counted as part of the village. It was a long rectangle, with the ends given over to animals, and the centre part used as the family's dwelling.

He had hardly stepped inside the door when he found an ale and a hunk of warm fresh bread pressed into his hands; both smelled delicious. He sat down and ate, Wallace and his wife and two of the older children joining him, apparently intrigued to have a visitor. They updated him on the health of their herd, and he simultaneously listened to the multiple smaller children who were running around and playing an imaginative game about warriors and sea monsters.

After a few minutes of small talk, trying not to seem rude, Donnell explained that he really needed to set out on a journey before noon, and moved the conversation on to the transaction. The gregarious sheep farmer's oats were not the best quality, but they were cheap, which was why Tarin had a standing arrangement to buy them.

Walking back out with two small sacks of oats looped together and tied through his belt, the sun had disappeared behind a cloud. As was so typical at this time of year, this was enough to make everything feel significantly colder, and for the wind to rise. At least it would cool the conditions for his walk uphill back home to Tarin's land and stable. And before long, he would be riding out on Beira's back, feeling the wind in his hair.

Donnell hadn't gone far, however, before he spotted a figure hurrying the other way – one whose outline he recognised instantly – squat, muscular, with one arm missing just below the elbow. He stopped, checking his footing, then hurried back up the way he had just came until he met Malcolm by the corner of the field.

Putting the sacks down for a moment, Donnell greeted his old friend.

Malcolm's clothes were plastered with sweat, and it seemed that he had hurried all the way from the nearby fishing village of Weir. He was also carrying a long-handled maul, a hammer-like tool with a three-foot haft, potentially useful as a weapon. Malcolm had forged the hammer during his own apprenticeship as a blacksmith, but Donnell hadn't seen it for many years – and it gave his friend a serious and warlike appearance.

"What news?" asked Donnell.

Malcolm took a moment to hook the maul into his belt, breathing hard as he did so. He then tugged at his mighty beard and looked Donnell in the eye. His face was flushed, his expression set and grim. "Norse raiders," he replied. "They mean war this time. Did you see the ships last night?"

"No." Donnell hesitated, glancing towards the sea and then back at his friend. It wasn't the first time that Malcolm had become alarmed at talk of Norse folk on the move, but months had passed, and so far the warnings had never amounted to anything. Was there something different this time?

"Where are they?" he asked his friend. "These Norse that you speak of. And what makes you think that they are raiders? The ones who have been seen further up the coast haven't done us any harm."

"That was all right when they stayed up the coast, Donnell." Malcolm was still slightly out of breath and appeared agitated. "But they are coming closer, now – moving warriors into position. Two ships have been on the move over the past day. Four others arrived two days ago. At first they made camp by the shore, a mile up the coast from Weir. I told the others that they should evacuate up to Cardhu, but they didn't listen."

"Go on."

"This morning, a great group of them arrived outside the village, fully armed, demanding that the locals provide them with food," Malcolm continued. "They wanted us to gather rocks to help them construct a fort, too. They call their leader Iohric the Ganger – he's a massive warrior, with lank white hair and a scarred face. They say that he got his name because he's too large to mount a horse."

"Wait – have they actually attacked Weir?"

"I think it's imminent, my friend. Iohric is gathering a group of troops outside the village, and more are on their way by all accounts. One of Alna's cousins is a man who knows the Norse and speaks their language. He went up to their camp to treat with them, but hasn't returned. Not that there's any love lost between me and him, but it's a worrying sign."

"Hmm, you are right about that," said Donnell, frowning deeply. "Unless it's possible that her cousin is stupid enough to have got lost."

Malcolm looked back in the direction of the shore, wincing slightly as he did so, and then nodded.

"There something else?" Donnell asked.

"Donnell, I think they'll take over the village, which means they will probably make slaves of any who resist. And now I'm starting to get really worried about Alna."

Donnell folded his arms as he looked at his old friend. Alna had been a cause of contention between them, and he didn't want to bring up that argument again. Indeed, the whole of Cardhu were suspicious of the folk of Weir – not least because they followed the new religion rather than respecting the traditional Celtic gods – and Malcolm's choice to go and live there had been frowned upon.

He also knew that his friend's decision had been strongly influenced by his growing infatuation with Alna. It was a match that the fisherfolk did not seem to approve of either. As for Alna herself, it was difficult to say. Malcolm certainly seemed to believe that his feelings were at least partly reciprocated. Donnell wasn't so sure.

"The Norse have kept to themselves for the most part," said Donnell at last, "and not bothered us over the past few months. Still, I think perhaps you should persuade Alna to get out of there and come up to Cardhu, just in case. She could stay with your father for a few days. I don't think they'd risk raiding up here…" He trailed off, looking back over his shoulder up at Cardhu, a village ringed with cliffs and trees, and with just three main points of approach, other than through the depths of Holm's Wood itself at the back of the settlement.

"I know," said Malcolm, "I've suggested the same thing. But she just laughs, and says there's no danger while she's with her family. I mean, yes, she does have a lot of cousins… but none of them are warriors."

"Unfortunately, Malcolm, as you know all too well, half of Alna's family are fools and the other half are worse than fools. Can't you… I don't know… just ask her to come visit or something, and then find reason to delay her here until the danger passes?"

Malcolm shook his head. "I don't think it would work. I mean, sure, I can try. But Donnell, can you help me? I can't protect her alone."

Donnell shrugged, somewhat unsure of what his friend was asking. They began to walk together towards the shore as they spoke, though Donnell intended to only go a part of the way before resuming his journey. "I don't think I'd be much help against a shipload of Norse," he said.

"You'd provide an extra spear, for one thing," said Malcolm.

"My fighting skills are very rusty. And as you know, I've mainly used my spear against forest animals. We're going to have to be civil, and settle this like the honest folk we are. As I said, the best way will be to get Alna away from any danger."

"I think she will listen to you, though," persisted Malcolm. "She laughed it off when I spoke to her of the risks that these raiders present."

"Perhaps," said Donnell, frowning again. "But listen, my friend – I'm under orders to deliver a message from the Laird to his brother over the next few days. I can't get involved – at least, not just now. After I return, I am happy to try…"

Malcolm stopped and clutched his longtime friend by the arm. "Do you really think we have that long to think and plan?" he asked. "Donnell, please. Surely you can take the time to walk down to Weir with me to talk some sense into the fisherfolk? Afterwards, I'll come up to Cardhu, and help you prepare for your journey more quickly."

Donnell hesitated. Going down to Weir and back would add a couple of hours to his journey at least. That meant setting out in the early afternoon, and not getting to the first stage of his destination until it got dark – perhaps all for nothing more than a bunch of fisherfolk in a panic over the sighting of a couple of Norse ships.

But then again, what if it was more than that? Was it worth the risk to his friend and to the folk of Weir – and those of Cardhu?

One way or another, Malcolm had always been there for him.

"Very well," he said at last, nodding and slapping his friend on the shoulder again. "Let's see if we can get through to the woman and her kinsfolk."

The First Attack

Together they made their way down the small trail at the edge of Wallace's drystane dyke. It came out on marshy land to the north of Weir itself, most of which was unpassable, but which featured a narrow and uneven rocky path between where they stood and the shore. It was difficult, muddy terrain, but they both knew it well, and also knew that when they reached the shore they would join the fine Lairds' Road which ran southwards down the coast to Wherrycross and eventually down to the Ayr Valley, or, to their right, all the way up to Inverkip in the north, where Tudorr ab Owain lived in a broch – a Hebridean round castle.

Indeed, northwards was the direction that Donnell was planning to go, but he wouldn't repeat this route for his journey – most of the path was unsuited to horses. Instead, he planned to leave on the main village road – which ran more or less directly between the Celtic Rock and the shore and Weir village – and he would then head north on the Lairds' Road.

The trail across the boggy wildlands itself was as muddy as they had expected, but they were able to pick their way along, and keep their boots dry in the main; fortunately the rains hadn't been too heavy so far this springtime. As they both knew, this area could be entirely waterlogged in fall. Birds were nesting among the long grasses and reeds; Donnell heard chicks calling for food, and saw lapwings –

unmistakable black feather crests upon the heads of the white-bellied birds – pecking for grubs in the distance. Any foragers that had come this way had missed those eggs, he thought, and so close to the village, too. Now the birds would aggressively defend their young from anyone who came close.

When they reached the road and squeezed carefully past a line of thorn bushes in flower, Malcolm stopped dead, looking in the direction of Weir.

And when Donnell stepped out beside him, he immediately saw why. At least twenty Norse warriors in full battle armour were striding along the coast road, not two dozen yards from them.

"Get back," Donnell hissed to his companion, and the pair stepped backwards off the road and crouched down behind the bushes.

The Norse were heading away from them and didn't appear to have noticed them yet, but it would only take a single one of the heathens to turn his head, and they would be seen for sure.

"They must have come from the long-fort," whispered Donnell. "And it looks like they are heading towards Weir, or perhaps Cardhu. Or both."

He glanced round at his friend, who was staring wide eyed, shocked at the sudden appearance of such a large troop of hostile warriors on their home soil. It was the sort of incursion that had often been talked about, but which neither of them had seen in their lifetimes.

Malcolm's fears were very well founded after all, he realised.

As a trained woodsman, Donnell was sure that he could trail the Norsemen stealthily along the road without being spotted. But could Malcolm? "Let's head back to the marsh," he said, "and follow them on the other side of the hedgerow," he said. "We'll get our feet wet, I know, but we'll avoid being seen." Malcolm nodded, and they rounded the thorn bushes back to the marshland, and began to tentatively walk along the narrow earthy strip. Malcolm went ahead; the bushes were to his right, and he was able to carefully hold on to leaves and twigs to keep his balance. As he followed, Donnell glanced down at the study maul looped into his friend's belt. It provided a sense of reassurance, but he knew it would be next to useless against that huge company of enemies.

Before long they had both managed to get the hang of walking on the rough surface without being too badly scratched by the thorns. They were maintaining a decent pace, not falling behind the Norsemen, but they weren't closing in either. Fortunately, the warriors didn't seem to be in a hurry. Indeed, they appeared to be in a relaxed, celebratory mood, laughing and engaging in occasional group chants and snatches of song.

They were now close to Weir. It was little more than a hamlet, Donnell knew – a ring of a dozen houses, as well as some outbuildings where fish and equipment were stored, and the remains of an ancient ruined fort. It had none of the farms that Cardhu did, and not nearly as many people, but it sat above a natural harbour, small but deep, with a sloping area of sand where boats could be drawn up and tied.

The warriors had come to a halt up ahead. Donnell stood on tiptoes; he heard shouts up ahead, but was unable to make out what was going on. He and Malcolm looked at each other, realising their helpless state – they couldn't easily make it back the way they came, and nor could they get past the warriors to warn the local villagers.

After what felt like a very long pause, there was further shouting up ahead. The voices were more urgent this time, it seemed to Donnell, though he knew nothing of the Norse language. Before long, four of the Norsemen hurried back the way they had come at a rapid pace, going right past where Donnell and Malcolm were sheltering. The men were carrying a wooden chest between them on a pair of sturdy ropes; they passed by without noticing their hidden observers.

He looked back to his left where the rest of the warriors were arrayed, and at that moment heard the unmistakable sound of a clashing of weapons. There were several shouts, and then a scream of pain, and a further agonised yell.

Cursing being so far back from the road, Donnell stretched forward from where he stood, deciding that he had to take the risk of looking out over the top of the bushes. When he did so, he saw that the Norsemen were now starting to charge towards Weir. And on the road, behind them, the bodies of two local men were lying in a pool of blood.

* * *

The pair of friends squeezed and pushed their way through a small gap in the bushes and hurried out, no longer caring about being seen.

Malcolm was just ahead of Donnell as they rushed over to the two prostrate figures, and he crouched and cradled one man's head in his huge calloused hand. Donnell knelt by the other victim, feeling for the man's pulse, while looking out towards the main group of Norsemen, who were still moving rapidly away.

"This one's dead," he told his friend.

The man who was being held by Malcolm had his eyes open, but they were flickering, and blood was flowing profusely from a wound in his chest. Donnell knew enough about injuries to tell that there was no recovery from this one – not unless, perhaps, the Mor-druids themselves were standing beside them, ready to intervene and cast a magical healing prayer to the goddess Brighid.

"Tadleigh, isn't it," said Malcolm gently, looking down at the man. "The great fisherman? Tell me – what happened? Why did they do this to you?" Donnell, glancing again at the retreating warriors, thought he already knew the answer, and was in no doubt that his friend did too. The Norse wanted to take over the village and make slaves of its inhabitants. None could stand in their way without coming to harm.

The man made a croaking noise, looking up to him, and trying and failing to speak. He tried once more, and then his head fell backwards against Malcolm, but he held out one arm and pointed towards the sea. It was enough.

A few minutes later, the big man stood on the rocks between the road and the coast, his front now covered in Tadleigh's blood. They had covered both men with their own cloaks, and pulled the bodies to the verge of the road where they were less likely to be disturbed, and could later be collected by their relatives – unless they, too, were killed by the raiders.

"That man Tadleigh was a gentle soul – quiet, kind-hearted," said Malcolm. "Never one to start a quarrel, or give anyone reason to harm him."

"They took something," said Donnell. "Loot perhaps?"

"In the chest? No, I don't think… I mean, whatever it was, there's no loot to be had in Weir. The people there have next to nothing beyond their fishing tackle."

"What was it then, do you think? Something they brought with them? They seemed to be in a hurry to move it."

"I don't know what that was. But one thing is for sure – the Norse are murderers, and nobody here is safe anymore."

"Yes – and I am sorry that I didn't listen to you sooner. You were right to be alarmed." Donnell glanced along the coastline as he spoke. "We need to get the message to the people of Weir. If we don't warn them, I fear that they will be enslaved or worse. But we can't fight our way past that horde of warriors."

"We could follow, and if the people are truly being attacked, lend our help."

Donnell glanced down. Back at the farm he had a fine spear, but he was currently carrying only a hunting knife. "True. But as I said before, I am not sure that one or even both of us would make enough of a difference. We should arm ourselves properly, and get a message to the Luftenand."

"That fool?" said Malcolm, and he spat. "I don't like or trust Ogledd."

"I don't like him either. But he has is the only one who can call for the Laird's help, and bring some actual warriors to aid us."

"Hmm." Malcolm patted the maul in his belt. "That would take too long. We're not empty-handed – we must do what we can."

"Against that many warriors, we really need the Laird's help. And also, Ogledd has the authority to muster all of the people in the village."

"Ach," said Malcolm, "but as I say – is there time?"

The pair of them looked towards Weir. For all of the noise and ferocity of the charge that they had witnessed, there had been no further screams or sounds of battle. It occurred to Donnell that the people of Weir would most likely surrender immediately, faced with such an overwhelming force. With luck, the people there would be unharmed for long enough for them to organise a rescue. He shared this thought with his friend.

Malcolm nodded at last, frowning deeply. "Very well," he said. "I will go up to speak with Ogledd myself, and persuade him of the danger." He pointed to his own chest. "Hopefully one look at all this blood will be enough to convince him. But I think we're going to need more than local warriors against this new threat. You know what the Norse are capable of – a single one of their longships has been known to destroy an entire village."

He leaned forward, and put his hand on Donnell's shoulder. "Can you take a message to the druids in Holm's Wood? They know who you are, and they have ways of protecting us, following the ancient traditions. I'd offer to go myself, but..." He trailed off, looking back towards Weir again.

"You don't want to be that far from Alna. I get it. But Malcolm, that would take me southwards towards Wherrycross. As I said, there's an important message that I've promised to deliver, and I need to ride north. I'm already late."

"Important?" Malcolm's face furrowed, and his dark eyes stared deep into Donnell's. "This is my home and my people we are talking about."

Donnell paused for a moment, studying his friend.

Home.

To him, home was Cardhu. But if Weir had fallen, then surely his own village was next in line for more of the brutality that they had just witnessed. And he would work for Tarin's farm forever than see that happen.

* * *

The rocks where they stood were well above sea level despite being close to the shore, and this vantage point allowed Donnell's grey eyes to take in the curving coastal route towards the town of Wherrycross, where the Laird had his seat, and the ridge of cliffs and Holm's Wood behind. He could make out the town in the distance before the distance blurred the view to his vision; he knew that it nestled on the shore, with the edge of the Holm's Wood forest behind, with its rich hunting grounds. The Laird and his men loved to sport for deer, although Donnell was sure that he knew the ways of the woodland better than the Laird ever would.

"What gives you the idea that the druids would get involved?" he said at last. "They protect the kingdom, yes, but they might see this as a local squabble."

"They'll do it. I *know* they will," said Malcolm, stepping closer. "You know as well as I do how much they do to protect us. Things would be a lot more dangerous here if not for their enchantments. It's their natural duty, using the power of the land and of great Lugh against outsiders. They have the kind of powers that can keep the people safe.

These enemy warriors have numbers, weapons, and even if the Laird brings in troops, they might just bring in even more. There's no doubt in my mind – we need to rely on the ancient power of the druids. It has always been there to protect us, quietly, hidden away."

Donnell chuckled slightly. "You're starting to sound like me." It was good, in truth, to hear Malcolm talk of the old ways, and of Lugh, the Celtic god of crafting – always the most revered of the deities among smiths. He had assumed that Malcolm's recent stay with the fisherfolk might have changed his values. "I thought you had started to follow the Weir folk, and believe in the one god like the Irish do."

Malcolm rolled his eyes. "I know what I've seen. Those crab eaters can believe anything they like." He wiped his brow with the back of his hand, which Donnell could see was still stained with blood. "So, will you go? I understand that it will interfere with your mission, and I am sorry."

"This is much more important, of course." Donnell said. "You are right. I need to ride out today, and perhaps Lugh will watch for me too, as he is known to protect travellers and messengers." He glanced the other direction. "Though on my return," he continued, "I don't know how I'm going to make it safely to the Laird's brother – from what we've seen, the Norse are active on the road, and I can't ride directly northwards without coming to their long-fort. I suppose I'll just come straight back to Cardhu…"

"… and take the footpath at the forest's edge, along to Eas Mòr," said Malcolm, finishing his friend's sentence.

"Yes. That's what I'll do."

"Thank you, Donnell. I think it's essential that we gain the power of the druids to help us. These are dark times."

"Well, my friend," Donnell said after a pause, slapping Malcolm's muscular back. "Let's make haste back up to Cardhu. I need to get the horse from Tarin's farm, or I won't be making it to the druids this day."

"You go on," said Malcolm, pulling his maul from his belt again, and raising it towards his chest. "I'm going to try to get Alna to safety first."

Donnell stared at him. "But what about the Norsemen? Malcolm, don't be a fool. You can't go close to there, not now with those warriors about. Please – come with me, and alert Ogledd."

"I will, as soon as I can. But first I will try to speak to her. You know I can't leave her in danger. I'll be safe – I am not going to charge in and attack. I know the rocks and caves along this coast better than anyone, you know I do. I can keep a low profile, I promise. And I will try to speak to as many of her family as will listen."

Donnell rubbed his stubbly chin, then shook his head slightly. "As you will."

"Yes. And as for Ogledd, leave him to me – don't waste time looking for the man."

"I am sure I can take a few minutes to find him. He was in the village earlier."

But Malcolm shook his head. "No. Just get your horse and set out. We need the druids' help as soon as possible. Once I've warned the people of Weir, I'll go straight to Cardhu myself to find the Luftenand."

Donnell patted the bags of supplies in his belt, looking down. "Very well. I'll tell Niamh that you are on your way, and then I'll fetch Beira from the farm."

"Stay safe, old friend."

"And you – don't do anything rash. I will find the druids, and beseech them for their help. Let us all hope that there is something they can do." Donnell began to walk away, and then paused one more time. "Malcolm, get out of there as quickly as you can."

"Thank you, Donnell." Malcolm blew out his bearded cheeks, and then waved the maul in the air briefly without a smile. "I will. With luck I will see you in Cardhu by the day's close, ahead of your journey north."

Donnell looked uphill at his route as he set off again. Holm's Wood ran in a strip all the way from the hills near Cardhu to Wherrycross and beyond, leaving only a strip of land between the trees and the shore itself – rocks, cliffs, and a bit of moorland. Most people never saw the druids, but he knew exactly where he had to go. And the day was getting progressively more complicated.

Into the Forest

Beira was restless. Donnell patted her flank, then gave her a bite of one of the turnips from the sack that had been left in the stable, leaving the rest for the other horses. The saddle bag of oats was now stuffed full from the supplies he had picked up at Wallace's farm, but they had a long way to go in the coming days, and he didn't want to use any just yet.

There was a sharp knock from outside. He turned and picked up the remaining bundles of dried fish which he kept prepared for travel, each one rolled into several folds of cloth and tied with flaxen cord; oats were all very well for the horse, but he needed something more to sustain him.

As he secured the food in the pouch beneath the saddle, he thought again of Malcolm, who often brought fish in crates up from Weir village. He worried for his friend's safety. He desparately hoped that Malcolm would be cautious like he had promised, rather than rushing into any confrontations.

The knock sounded again, but Donnell was not going to be interrupted from his preparations – it was important not to miss anything vital. He strapped his hunting spear below the saddle, a sturdy weapon with a similar blade to a battle spear, but of only around five feet in length, making it handier for use within the forest. He also checked his small supply of silver groats. Finally, satisfied that all was ready, he stroked Beira's ears, closed and locked the door that led to his own tiny sleeping quarters at the back of the stable building, then led the chestnut-coloured steed gently by the reins to the entrance.

As he expected, it was Tarin outside. The man was the wealthiest farmer in the village, and owned the stable that Donnell slept in – the one benefit he received in exchange for working the horses and a dozen other labouring tasks as he paid off his family debt. The man was scowling at having to wait. There was no politeness in his knocking, Donnell knew – Tarin could have walked in at any point, but the man detested the animal smell of the barn. As a farmer, Tarin was unusual in that he could afford to pay others to do his labour – not through the fruits of his own work, Donnell knew, but because his father and grandfather had left the property to him. Tarin therefore lived in a fine longhouse with several outbuildings including the stable itself, and had hopes of becoming the village Luftenand one day.

"The Luftenand left something here for you," said Tarin sourly, passing Donnell a small slip of parchment.

Donnell placed the message inside the pocket of his jerkin and patted the outside of the garment. "Good. You can tell him I received it."

Tarin glanced behind him, staring at Beira with his nose wrinkled. "You're not taking that beast out, are you? We need it on the fields today." Tarin's face was thin and heavily bearded, and he had a pinched, mean look to his eyes.

Donnell patted Beira again, out of habit. "Aye," he said, only glancing briefly at the older man, and then looking past him as if casting an eye out at the weather. "That message you gave me comes from the Laird, and needs delivered urgently. On the orders of his huntsmaster, Macswain."

"Well." Taken aback, Tarin opened and closed his mouth several times, looking around and clenched his long hands together as he thought of a response. "You'll have to hurry, then. We need all three horses later today. Now that the tide is going out, I want you to gather the sea harvest up. One of Niamh's offspring is coming to help spread the seaweed it on the fields tomorrow."

Donnell was silent for a moment, now looking down towards Weir. The sea looked calm from what they could see, with two low hills in between where they stood and the shore – it would have been a fine day for such work, if the grim and deadly events had not intervened.

He swung himself up into the saddle. "That's a pity, goodman," he said, looking at Tarin directly again. "As I need to use Beira for several days. I have to travel to give this to the Laird's brother in the north. It's a serious matter, apparently, but not for your ears." He patted his jerkin pocket again as he spoke.

Tarin took a breath and stepped back, looking up at Donnell without having to crane his neck. "Then you can't take that horse with you. I can't do without it. The Laird will have to provide a different mount from his stables at Wherrycross. We need all three of ours, so it's only reasonable."

Donnell looked at him and sighed, impatient to get moving. "Tarin, I understand this, but really, I can't spare the time to go for another horse, if they would even give me one. I'll need to ride her north today. You know, I don't think this will turn out to be an afternoon for gathering sea harvest anyway – a storm is on its way from across the water."

"That is *my* horse," Tarin said, changing tack in his approach to thwarting Donnell. "You can't take it. I tell you again – you'll have to ask the Laird for a mount."

"Listen – if you just let me ride out on Beira, I will be much quicker in delivering my message, and quicker getting back here and back to work as well. It's the Laird's orders, remember."

"Donnell, I insist. My fields cannot wait."

"Aye," said Donnell. "I will certainly have to make haste." Nudging the horse's flanks with his knees and edging past Tarin, Donnell pulled her round so that the mare's backside was pointing towards the farmer. "I'll do my best to be persuasive when I get to my destination."

He shook the reins, and Beira broke into a canter as he made his way to the edge of the farm. Not caring to look back, they leaped the nearest fence, and were away. His heart thumping with exhilaration, Donnell patted the chestnut mare's side, and breathed deeply of the salty coastal air.

* * *

Tarin's farm was on the north side of most of the houses and crofts of Cardhu, and from there it was possible to go directly towards the edge of the forest without passing through the main part of the village. Donnell therefore made his way past the backs of the last few homesteads of Cardhu, and followed a wide, little-used path that connected the village with the nearby hills. To the right were the stony half-walls of a few abandoned crofts from generations back; the land around them was ridged with ancient middens, and no use for crofting nowadays.

After a few minutes, the way narrowed into a stony former footpath that had long since been broken up by tree roots, and then began to descend. He could see the shoreline and the distant outline of the fishing village of Weir off to the right. He knew he could follow this path all the way to the shore in the shadow of a long, low line of inland cliffs, rising above the rough, infertile grasslands that sloped down to the coast.

However, instead of doing so, he planned to find a pass that would lead him through the hills and up to top of the ridge of cliffs, near the forest's edge. From there, the rocky surface formed a natural path, suitable for riding. Donnell preferred the open land and the forest to travelling by road, and could make his way around quickly without needing a map. And the trees of Holm's Wood and the secret places of the druids would be easier to access from atop the cliffs than from down at the shore.

Ahead, the route above the cliffs ran southwards nearly as far as the town of Wherrycross itself, and he would need to travel for most of that distance. He would only enter the forest when he was closer to his destination, for its paths were not well suited to horses.

He was content to have let Tarin believe that he was obeying the instruction to find an alternative mount, but he had no intention of doing so. As soon as he had spoken to the druids, he would ride directly back north, following the edge of the forest.

Of course, his detour would take the time on to the evening, making it very late before he could make for Inverkip with the Laird's message. He might even need to ride overnight. But Beira was a fine horse, and he was confident that he could make up the time, completing the main part of the journey as quickly as possible. Just as long as he could avoid facing Tarin on his return, and the need to come up with yet another account of his own movements.

As Beira's hooves started to click on the harder grounds that marked the beginning of the stony ridge, he looked up. He knew the way – he had been there many times before – but the first part would be awkward on horseback. Every so often along the rocks of the cliff a way through could be found, where the blocky sandstone had collapsed at some point or another. Some of these had been used as paths for many a generation. But few were suitable for him now.

Ignoring the first such pass, Donnell rode Beira hard along the rock-strewn grasslands at the foot of the cliffs until he reached one of the largest such gaps in the rock, and dismounted. Here the fallen sandstone had landed kindly, providing a wide pathway of slabs of rock that were hardly overgrown at all, even at the height of summer.

Even so, it was difficult to lead Beira up this way, and she initially resisted, pulling back hard. Knowing that he couldn't force her to move, he stopped for a moment, calming himself, and stroking the chestnut horse on her flank and neck. She whinnied and calmed, and they were ready to move forward once more.

Reaching the top, the opening widened out, and he could see signs of the passing on foot of a few travellers of one kind or another, but these soon disappeared. Donnell led Beira by hand, slowly, along the tops of the cliff rocks for another few hundred paces. He looked down from time to time; they were high above the marshy scrublands, and he could see Wherrycross town much more clearly up ahead. The town itself was a place he rarely visited these days, despite it being the largest settlement in the area.

It was now well into the afternoon. In his head, he pictured Norsemen streaming up from the coast, axes in hand, smashing through the houses of Cardhu. Feeling an unfamiliar tension thoughtout his body, he mounted up again, and hurried on.

There was a single ship heading towards Wherrycross, though it didn't look like a Norse vessel. A trader from down the coast at Ayr, perhaps, or even from over in Ulster, the lost part of his home kingdom, now overrun by Irishmen and Norse.

He rode on for another hour, until clumps of the tangled whin bushes started to appear around them, and Donnell cut inland, knowing that Beira could easily step over these without concern for the thorns. Ahead, the nearest rows of trees were sparse, but it wouldn't be long before the forest closed in, and a general deep green gloom was starting to fill the edge of his vision.

He paused, scanning the tree line, before spotting a slightly recessed area, where the ground in front of a group of young trees was a little clearer than its surroundings. That was the place – the beginnings of the path he needed to take. It had been a long time, but he was sure of it. Beira whinnied and he patted her again, and began to make directly for the forest.

As he passed through the first clump of trees at the edge of the forest, thin birches with the first full spring leaves of the palest green upon them, he pondered over the arrival of Norseman on the coast. They had controlled the isles of Arran and Bute for more than a generation, but hadn't shown an interest in raiding the mainland in recent memory, and trade flowed between his people and theirs periodically. This new development was a worrying sign, he thought – a tribal split among the heathens, perhaps, or a recently rekindling of their natural bloodlust. It was not without warning, mind. Since he was a child, he had heard tales and warnings of ferocious armies of Norsemen. Their brooding presence had always been there, across the water. And more recently, folk from the south had come bearing tales of wars, raids, and towns falling to the numberless enemy.

The forest around him was getting denser now, and the path less even, but still wide enough for him to guide the horse along. It was mercifully free from rocks, but some trees branches on either side forced him to duck down as he rode.

He had been riding for the best part of an hour when he pulled Beira to a stop, and reached down for a waterskin from beside the saddle. Taking a deep swig, he looked around. It couldn't be far now, he thought, though he hadn't approached from this direction before. It was already late, and he didn't want to be deep in the forest after dark.

Just then, he heard some cackling noises from the depths of the forest further on. Fixing the water securely back in its place, he loosened the hunting spear and lifted it, holding it in his right hand and taking the reins with just his left. He nudged Beira's sides and she walked on steadily further along the path, as he sat and glanced every which way, silent and vigilant.

A small rock flew down out of nowhere, bouncing just ahead of Beira's front hooves, and she shied.

There were boggles lurking among the trees, Donnell was sure of it.

The monstrous sprites were known to harass lone travellers, and were reckless and violent in their habits, if not always entirely evil. Proceeding slowly and carefully was unlikely to help – it made it easier for him to avoid hazards, but also presented an easier target to the creatures. But he was loath to go too fast on horseback – the path was narrow and rough, and its carpet of dead pine needles could conceal all manner of ills.

He might not have any choice.

As another stone bounced beneath the horse's legs, Donnell pressed his heels to Beira's flanks.

Druid Stones

They hurried on, ducking under branches as they cantered across the soft rooted ground. Thin, supple pine branches were whipping him in the face now, and he held the spear up in front of him to provide a modicum of protection, and peered forward as he rode.

Further ahead, numerous small dark figures seemed to be clambering on branches. Something was hanging down – a vine, or trailing ivy? No – it was a net!

Donnell pulled up the reins sharply and veered off to the left, bashing his arm against a tree which was mercifully thin and willowy and which gave way slightly at the impact. He had narrowly missed having his head and upper body entwined in the net trap.

Twisting round in a half circle, he guided Beira around in a loop to avoid the way that was blocked. He slowed slightly and then surged forward, approaching the same point from another angle.

And then, suddenly, he found himself in the clearing that he had been looking for. It contrasted so sharply with the gloom of the trees before that it was hard to imagine that both places were within the same forest. It was like coming in from a dark, cold night into a well-lit inn taproom.

The area ahead was centred on a rocky knoll or mound, with a very large treeless area all around. A small lochan lay below the knoll, with the edge of the forest beyond visible more distantly. The area was known to Donnell, but he had never come into it before, for it was revered as a sacred place.

As he came closer, he saw that the knoll was partially hollowed out, leading to a bowl-shaped formation, in which were several mysterious buildings, rather like small houses with pointed roofs, but six-walled and painted in multiple colours. Each was slightly different in size and shape, and there were carved wooden totems in front and between them, mostly of animal figures.

Five familiar people were there, each wearing their usual very plain patched robes. The druids. Two were crouching near a rock-ringed fire close by, and they stood and looked up at Donnell as he emerged. He could make out the other three on carved tree stumps by the knoll at the far side of the settlement; they comprised the flame-haired healer Fenella, a male druid strumming quietly at a lute, and a woman who was smoking a long pipe. They looked to him more relaxed and ordinary – more human, even – than when they came to the village for the ancient ceremony every Samhain.

The two nearer druids stood and walked over. One narrowed his eyes slightly at first, and then nodded his head. "Welcome," he said simply, although without any particular warmth. Donnell recognised him as Congal, leader of the druid circle with whom he had briefly spoken at Samhain.

"I'm pleased to see you all here," said Donnell hoarsely, gesturing around, then cleared his throat. "I worried that you might be travelling, or otherwise preoccupied." He realised that his heart had been pounding after escaping the trap, and he looked behind him to check for signs of pursuit as he dismounted.

He walked towards the two men, leading the horse behind him. Congal took the reins from him, speaking to Beira quietly in words from the old tongue, and moved away slightly to secure the beast's reins to a withered tree stump, leaving his fellow druid to continue the conversation.

"I suppose you have come here with a message for us?" Gabrán was shorter than his companion, with straight jet-black hair and eyes so vividly amber that they appeared to glow slightly.

"Yes and no," replied Donnell. "There is trouble abroad, where I live. But I see that this area is also unsafe." He pointed behind him. "I was harassed by boggles on my way, and barely escaped. I think they may be waiting in the trees for my return."

"Yes. But please, do not worry too much about our mischievous neighbours," said Gabrán. "They know that this is not their domain. In fact..." Gabrán shifted his robes slightly; as he did so, he revealed a small golden brooch with an amber gemstone in the centre, and intricate carvings of deer and eagles. He unpinned it, and spun it several times on the palm of his hand. A thin bright line of yellow light began to emerge until there was a glowing column rising several feet above the man. Then with an outward gesture with both hands by the druid, the light shot out in a semi-circle, breaking into a thousand small star-like fragments like sparks from a fire, and blasting through the trees around them in all directions. Donnell heard shrieks of pain and anger among the treetops.

"That should send a clear message, I think," Gabrán said slowly, replacing the brooch on his patched robes, and covering it up, "about how we like our visitors to be treated. Now, please sit."

* * *

The pipe-smoking druid, a woman with waist-length blonde hair streaked with silver, had approached them. Placing her pipe down, she rolled a large round of tree trunk over to where they stood, turned it onto its end as a stool, then gestured to Donnell. He sat, looking round to check on Beira, who was now slurping contentedly from a water trough that Congal had brought over, near where her reins had been tied. The woman then brought another log round over to the fire for herself.

He took a deep breath, glad to finally be safe, and then began to speak. "You may remember Malcolm…" he said, and was then interrupted.

"Yes, the blacksmith boy," said the blonde druidess, who was now sitting opposite him.

"No, Méabh," replied Gabrán, looking at her as he crouched down beside them. "He stopped all that and went to live in Weir."

"Ah. So, he became a fisherman."

"Not from what I heard. He can't manage a boat – water is not his domain," Gabrán replied, shaking his head slightly.

"Well, he lost his arm in the forge when he was little more than a child, poor lad. No wonder he can't catch fish."

"Or swim."

"Malcolm, son of the smith? He lost his heart to a fisherman's wife, I heard," put in the red-haired Fenella, who had now approached the group, together with the lute playing druid, Loarn.

Congal held up his hands for calm. Donnell noted that unlike his comrade Gabrán, he was not wearing a brooch under his robes. "Just let the man speak, my brothers and sisters," he said.

Donnell cleared his throat again, and resumed. "Malcolm, as you've said," he nodded at Gabrán and Méabh, "lives with the fisherfolk of Weir village. Recently, he tells me, Norsemen have set up a long-fort along the short nearby, and threatened the local people. I myself saw two full-sized Norse warships, the kind that came with the Norwegian king when he visited all those years ago, and then saw a company of armed warriors marching on Weir earlier today."

Loarn, the lute player, nodded and clicked his teeth. "Worrying," he said, in a voice that sounded rather detached from the issue. He was standing a few paces away, not looking at the group, and was playing with the tuning on his lute. The fifth druid had an unfocused look to him, Donnell thought. Perhaps it was the large grey beard which was smeared with the remnants of food and grease, or the way that his eyes were large, dark shadowed and heavily lined, as if he slept poorly.

"It needn't mean much, on its own," cautioned Congal.

"Well, I think the young man has a point," said Loarn, still plucking at the strings.

It wasn't going well, Donnell realised.

"So, um…" he continued. "We were thinking, well. Perhaps you could help the people. They respect and rely on you. Is there something you can do to protect or shield them? They are defenceless."

"Your worry for them is commendable," said Méabh, frowning. "But do not let it define you."

"Still," said Fenella. "We must do something."

"We cannot just fight off the Norsemen," said Gabrán. "We are not warriors or generals – not like the druids of old, who would lead armies into battle."

"But we are defenders," said Fenella, her red hair catching the afternoon light as she stepped closer to the fire. "Or at least, we should be."

"We defend the land," replied Gabrán, looking up at his companion. "But we cannot decide who rules and who does not. It was our ancient mistake to get involved in the wars in Ireland."

Donnell glared at Gabrán for a moment. This was not what he expected – not what Malcolm and all the folk of the coast needed from their druids. He recalled momentarily that Gabrán had not been present at the most recent visit of the druids to Cardhu, during the annual Samhain festival.

Before Donnell had thought about this any further, however, Congal, the leader, placed his hand on Gabrán's shoulder to and indicated that the man should now hold his peace. He then held up both of his hands in for the quiet and attention of the group once again. As he did so, Donnell noticed that the man also had a sparking gemstone not unlike the amber stone, but that it was fashioned into a ring on his hand, rather than a brooch. The gem was circular, white, and set in gleaming silver. In all the visits of the druids to Cardhu, he had never seen this before.

"My friend," said Congal, looking down at the crouching Gabrán, "we can trust young Donnell of Cardhu, of that I am sure, but let us not bring him into complex and disturbing questions such as these, about who our circle of Mor-druids should help, and when. He has already seen and heard rather too much, today." With a slight nod, Gabrán stood and took a pace back from the circle.

"Traveller," Congal continued, now looking at Donnell, "people move around, they build, they fight, and times move on. We are protectors of this land, that's true, but is not our business to decide which people hold one village or area of the coast, even if they choose to wrest it from another. And it certainly not our place or within our means to fight wars, even justified ones, or to build defences for people who have overlooked the maintenance of their own. Those days are gone. Now we seek to work with nature and in harmony with the great gods themselves."

"Aye, but… the people of Cardhu are peace-loving folk, you must know that. They have animals and children. Will you not do something to help? I'm not wishing any harm on the Norsemen, just… well, I thought that you could perhaps protect the village. Ward them off somehow."

"Perhaps we could, and perhaps we couldn't," replied Congal. "These Norse have gods and magics of their own. They don't follow our ways."

"I know," said Donnell. "It's well known that they are savages who take slaves, and murder children for sport."

A few of the group muttered, and the red-headed Fenella shook her head vigorously. "You're wrong about them. I've spoken to the Norse folk over on Arran, and for the most part they are people just like yourselves, with farms and families."

"I, too, have spoken with the Norse," said Gabrán quietly.

"Their farmers are fine, I'm sure," said Donnell, now standing up as he looked at the druidess. "But they are not like us. They burned down a house – and we saw them slay two men from Weir. It was an unprovoked attack."

Fenella nodded slowly without replying, a look of concern on her face.

"Perhaps such attacks were unprovoked," put in the leader Congal, "or perhaps not. It is not really for us to judge that from our seat here." He gestured to Fenella to untie Beira. "We will give it some thought, Donnell, but I suggest that you take it up with your Laird or the knights of the realm. Those are the proper authorities if a crime has been committed. Let the rulers carry out the King's justice, and we will work to protect the land, as is our sacred duty."

Donnell looked again to Loarn, the one out of the five who had unambiguously spoken up in his favour, but the fifth druid now had his back to them, and was playing his lute and singing very softly under his breath. Donnell noticed that the man's cloak was ripped in several places, with twigs and leaves caught in the rents.

Fenella, the healer druidess, had untied Beira, and she led the horse over as Donnell walked back to the edge of the clearing. She patted and spoke softly to the animal as she came, and Beira seemed most content. "Beautiful horse you have here, traveller," she said, handing Donnell the reins. "Look after her. Fare well and quickly – the afternoon is getting on. I'm sure I don't need to tell you that Holm's Wood can be a dangerous place by night."

"Yes. Thank you."

"No need for any thanks, but…" She glanced round at her comrades, and then looked back at Donnell. "Believe me – I have heard and understood what you had to say."

He nodded, took the reins from the druidess, and then turned towards the trees.

At the Cliffs

The sun was descending towards the sea in the west when Donnell emerged from the trees, cursing the recalcitrance of the druids.

On some level, he had suspected from the start that they would refuse. But what use were all of their powers if they wouldn't use them for the common good, he asked himself? Put the fear of damnation into some boggles if it suits them, it appeared, or just as a demonstration of power, but not get involved in anything more complex than protecting birds and trees, and doing their annual rituals.

Maybe the other villagers were right to neglect the old ways, and treat Samhain as an excuse for drinking and carousing. Granted, two of the druids had been more positive about his message. But the majority, and in particular the leader Congal, had carried the day. And that meant that the druids would stay in the forest, and leave the folk of Weir to their fate.

He had failed.

Looking both ways, Donnell briefly flirted with the idea of going straight back to Cardhu and helping to warn the village himself, but decided against it. Malcolm would surely be there by now, and his friend was still generally well liked and trusted – more so than he was himself as a mere farmer's bondsman, he was sure. The village folk were in danger, undoubtedly, but once again, there was little that one man could do.

Besides, to delay any further with the Laird's message that he was sworn to deliver would be to court severe punishment. Laird Cennaid ab Owain of Wherrycross and Cunninghame was not known for his moderation or his patience, and Donnell had long ago fallen from his good graces by leaving the huntsmaster's service and returning to work on Tarin's farm. No – he would have to make for Inverkip without further delay – he would ride due north overnight. Perhaps when he got there, he would find the Laird's brother willing to listen to his concerns, and even to offer some aid.

He intended to follow the edge of the forest as far as possible on his way northwards towards Inverkip. However, he now had some time to make up. Accordingly, the best approach would be to first make his way down to the Lairds' Road that hugged the coast, and then circle back and make a good pace up the road itself or the beach alongside as he headed back north towards Cardhu. That would mean a cautious ride down to the road itself, however, and he would have to navigate past the cliffs again before he could reach it.

Hurrying out towards the clifftops, Donnell urged Beira into a trot, staying well clear of the edge. The going was good here, he knew – the tops of the sandstone cliffs providing a better path than he would find on most village roads – and they trotted on for several hundred paces before another stone came flying in his direction. This time it didn't merely rattle towards his horse's legs, but was fired at pace, whistling narrowly past his head. He cursed, and urged Beira forward more quickly. He could now make out three boggles, small, greenish creatures with bat-like ears. Their limbs were so skinny and dark that superstitious villagers sometimes took them for child skeletons, risen from the grave to gain revenge.

Another stone shot out, and this time he felt a sharp pain in his lower back. The boggles were skulking in the bushes, then leaping out and firing pebbles with slingshots and catapults. With no helmet on, there was no doubt in Donnell's mind at all that a direct hit to his head had a chance of cracking his skull. A further boggle stood just ahead on his path, and he slashed out at it with his hunting spear as he rode forward. It ducked and scuttled away into the bushes.

The cliffs were getting lower to his right, and within a few hundred more paces he could get away from this exposed plateau and head for the shore. He patted Beira's neck and hunkered down low over her back; another rock whizzed past, and a second caught harmlessly against his cloak and then fell down to one side.

The horse cantered on across the rocky surface, and Donnell began to get the impression he was leaving the boggles behind. But then… what was that up ahead? If he was not mistaken, a group of the evil creatures were waiting behind the last huddle of sandstone rocks, exactly where he had been planning to turn and head down towards the road. Was this another trap? It certainly looked that way.

On impulse, he pulled Beira to the right, crashing through a large stand of whin bushes. A boggle rolled out of the way of the flailing hooves, its mean little face suddenly terrified. On the other side of the whins, among the limited cover of bushes and a few birch saplings, the rocks were no longer flying in his direction, and he slowed. If he remembered correctly, there was one last navigable path leading down before the end of the cliffs, though it would be a difficult climb whilst leading an already frightened horse, and while under fire. But what choice did he have?

They trotted on until he saw it. A v-shaped crevasse in the top of the cliffs clearly marked the spot where a section of rock had collapsed centuries before. He had climbed up and down that spot as a child many times; it was steep, but should be possible even for Beira as long as he led the horse, and took things slowly and carefully.

He spurred Beira forward to the edge, hearing some gleeful shrieks as he came into sight of his attackers once again. He dismounted, praying that the boggles were out of range, or that they would simply take a while to load up their slings again; they hardly seemed to be the finest marksmen, anyway. But they were approaching, stalking him in a pack. He raised the hunting spear high above his head as he stepped forward, hoping that this might make them draw back, wary of attacking, and there was a moment of calm as the creatures drew back. Then Donnell rapidly strapped the spear back underneath the saddle so that he would have a hand free while holding the reins, and took his first steps down into the crevasse.

* * *

A small rivulet of water running down the rocks caused Donnell to slip slightly as he first stepped down, but he quickly regained his footing. Beira was reluctant, but Donnell used his most commanding voice to urge her on, and she took a step forward. Below them, after four more ledges, there was a marshy area of ground, with a deserted-looking wooden shack off to one side. To the other side was a tumbledown fence roughly delineating a square, with a small lochan at the near edge, its waters catching the fading glimmer of sunlight from the west. He would aim to strike a path in-between the shack and the water.

Half slipping, half walking, the pair made their way down to the foot of the pass. As he reached the last slab of fallen rock, Donnell looked up, and saw that at least half a dozen pairs of beady eyes were there, staring down at them – though not shooting. He'd got lucky, it seemed – perhaps they were out of missiles, or had simply been flummoxed by his sudden change of direction. Muttering a quick prayer of thanks to the Celtic gods, he led the horse away from the rockfall and out into the marshland.

Donnell couldn't resist a quick glance at the tumbledown homestead as he led the horse past. If he wasn't mistaken – and he was sure that he was right – this was where old master Eochaid had once lived. As children, Malcolm and Donnell had been slightly fearful of the old man, with his books and potions and wild pronouncements about the state of knowledge and magic. Most other folk were wary of him indeed, no doubt partly due to his deformity – one of the old man's hands looked like that of a lizard, brown and scaled and with claws instead of fingertips. However, the children had found this more curious than worrying.

Eochaid was known to be a spellcaster, interested in creatures of the air and water such as kelpies and brollachan, and sometimes rumoured to be a shapeshifter, too. Donnell had found him fascinating.

Later, in their teenage years, both he and Malcolm had met Eochaid once again, and had come to know and trust the old spellcaster. Malcolm in particular had always been curious about the man's books and learning. The old man seemed to have a form of his own wisdom and power, quite different to that of the druids, and was rumoured to be a master of illusions. If only he was here now to help ward off the boggles. But to the best of Donnell's knowledge, Eochaid had long since left to live in the North – almost ten summers ago, now.

Ahead, the way between the shack and the broken-down fencing was muddy and rutted. There were some small deep footprints here and there demonstrating how soft the mud was, and Donnell tried to skirt round the edge of this morass, keeping close to the fence and placing one hand on it as he walked. But he had to walk away from it at the point that a massive puddle blocked the way, running from the fenced field to the open area. Some planks had been laid down to the right of this, on the same side as the shack, and as he stepped from the fence he walked upon those to keep his boots away from the worst of the mud. And then he found himself falling, Beira's reins slipping from his grasp.

He managed to grasp one of the planks with both hands, and dangled there for a moment, looking around and down. Below, a sharpened spike pointed up from the small, crude pit, and as he fell, he twisted his body to avoid it, then landed with a splash in knee-deep stinking water. He heard a whinny and the sound of galloping footsteps – Beira had wisely decided to make a break for it.

The same beady eyes appeared at the edge of the pit above him, leering down.

He really hated boggles.

* * *

He had been tied up competently enough.

Donnell couldn't remember what the creatures had done to cause him to lose consciousness, but since he had come to his senses, his attempts to stretch either arm around from behind his back had been unsuccessful, and wiggling them didn't seem to loosen the bonds. Nor could he separate his legs or kick out. Fortunately, he could still feel his fingers and toes.

He was being carried by a gang of chattering boggles, at least half a dozen of the little creatures. They had lashed three branches through his bonds in order to make six makeshift carry handles, and were carrying him face up with surprising strength and pace. They were now deep in the woods again, and despite his years of travelling in these parts, nothing around looked familiar, and his attempts to get his bearings were not helped by the fact that it was now getting dark. With his horse and supplies nowhere in sight; he dearly hoped the animal would just return home to the farm, where with luck the idiot Tarin would take her in for the evening. Or, more likely, one of the wiser villagers such as Niamh would notice.

And as for his own fate… it was said that boggles at times ate human flesh. Perhaps, as the druid Fenella had just said of the Norsemen, that was only a myth. Unfortunately, that hope felt over-optimistic under the circumstances.

The creatures didn't seem to want him dead immediately, at least, but they clearly delighted in tormenting him. Every so often one of them would prod him with a sharpened stick, which not only cut him painfully, it stung like ant venom. His yelps of distress caused the whole group to break into a high-pitched giggling. They really were vile creatures, he thought to himself.

"Hoy, you little monsters," he shouted. "I'll give you silver if you let me go." They were quiet for a moment, then burst into giggling and chattering again. One of them prodded a stick towards his mouth, and he was only just able to move his head enough to stop the sharp point going in. He felt it scrape across his cheek, and the pain flared.

"Ow!" he screamed. "Let me down, you swine-loving dung eaters!" They giggled some more, and bounced him up and down upon the branches.

The trees above were large now; he saw huge oak boles and branches all around, and the sky above had almost fully darkened. Even if he got away from the creatures, he was in deep trouble. From what he knew, this part of Holm's Wood must be near the South or East, where the oldest oaks could still be found, the greatest ones close to the coast having been long since cut for timber. There were wolves here, too, and if they were attacked and the boggles had to flee, he knew who would be left behind as food.

The boggles had slowed slightly, whether struggling under the weight or due to the darker conditions. Their eyes glowed in the gloom, and he tried to raise his head to see what was going on. If he had reached their home, he was finished – he'd be sliced up and eaten fresh.

And suddenly, he found himself on the ground, pain spreading across his back, from a rock, root, or some other object. The boggles were making different sounds now – low, agitated whoops. They were spinning around and waving their sharp sticks, and he saw one pull out its slingshot.

Caelia

An arrow shot through the air not more than a foot above his face and embedded itself into the nearest tree bole. What followed was a minute or so of screeching and chaos, during which he was stepped upon several times as boggles dashed about.

When silence finally fell, a slight figure leaned over him, smiling, and then with three rapid fire movements of a blade, slit the bonds that held him. He sat up, rubbing his arms, just then realising that the pain from when he was dropped came largely from the tree branch under his shoulder blades, one of the three that were being using to carry him.

He peered through the twilight and made out the face of his saviour. "Caelia," he cried out in sudden recognition. He had played with the strange girl many years before as a child, and had last seen her in the early days of his apprenticeship to the huntsmaster. Caelia was one of the forest folk, and had not grown any taller since then; she stood not much more than four feet off the ground. Her shoulders were powerful, her hair was long, golden, and braided into several plaits, all tucked into her belt. Her leather clothing was closely fitted and sewn in strange diamond-shaped and triangular sections.

"I suppose you owe me your life," she said, slipping her long, straight hunting knife back into a sheath at her belt. "It's most likely that they would have killed you tonight. Although sometimes they like to make it last a bit longer."

"Thank you, so, so much," he mumbled, not quite sure what to make of this. "It is Caelia, right? Do you remember me?"

"Hmm… I'm quite annoyed with you, actually," she said, now looking at the short, double-curved bow that she had been using, checking the string carefully for damage, and then slinging it back across her shoulders. Then she smiled. Her face was entirely a reddish brown as if made of nothing but freckles, wide around the cheeks and narrow at the chin, and her eyes were large and green. "You stopped coming to play here. Where have you been?"

Donnell heaved himself to his feet, his body a kaleidoscope of pain; whichever way he moved, new combinations of aches would swim into his consciousness. He reached out and patted her gently on the upper arm. "Thank you again, Caelia. And I…" He hesitated. "The thing is, I don't exactly play anymore. It's been… it's been years. I have to work now, you know – look after the horses on Tarin's farm, and so on. Talking of which, I don't suppose you've seen my horse? A mare, chestnut brown, sleek and beautiful. I've lost her."

"Well, it doesn't sound like you're so good at your job," she said, then threw her head back and gave a gurgling laugh. "Well, it's nice to see you, Donnell, even if you are too old now, and have forgotten how to have fun. Come on – we are far too close to Boggle's Hame here."

She leapt up in a single movement, and broke into an easy, swift-footed run. Donnell spurred his aching body on to follow. Caelia did look like little more than a child up ahead of him. And then she swung herself up and ran along the top of a low branch like a squirrel. Definitely not a child, he thought.

* * *

They ran on for some time, Caelia leaping from branch to rock, and running on the ground only for around half of the time. She occasionally looked back as if to check on him, but then more times than not she winked or made a silly face. He felt much reassured to be with her, all the same – he would otherwise be entirely lost, and the route that she was following stayed perfectly smooth and easy to run on. As far as he could tell from what could be seen of the night sky, they were heading westward.

After a while she slowed, and the forest around seemed to be thinning. He heard a wolf howl in the distance, and some birds, disturbed, fluttered around above them and then settled. She turned, and let Donnell catch up. "We're getting close to where the armoured people were hunting today," she said. "You know them, right? More boring people like you who don't know proper games." She grinned.

"Right. It could have been the Laird and his households," he said. "And some of the knights and guests from his Hall, no doubt."

"If you say so." She narrowed her eyes, and then, in a smooth move, flipped the knife out of her belt again and lunged forward. A lone boggle was standing there, and suddenly found himself pinned back against a tree with one of Caelia's hands clutching his shoulder and her knife point at his throat. Donnell noticed that he was wearing a dark blue cloak, not like the rags worn by the others that had recently attacked him.

"Spy," snarled Caelia. "What do you want?"

"No, I'm no spy! I am innocent!" answered the creature in a rasping voice. "Spare me, please."

"Tell me why I should spare your life, besides the displeasure of having to clean your dirty blood from my blade?"

The boggle shrank back even further against the tree trunk. "I was just passing through, your worship. I have an errand to run, to the human town. No, don't think because of my looks that I am one of those cutthroats who live in the woods. I am just a humble wanderer, making my way past. I'm no murderer, or thief, or spy."

"Hmm." Caelia pulled the knife back, and the small creature relaxed his body somewhat. "Rather too well dressed to be a wanderer, if you ask me, but you also don't have the look of that bandit tribe, true enough." She stood back and sheathed the knife. "Get on your way then, creature. But if I see you here again then you will meet the punishment of a spy."

The boggle turned and ran without another word, his small blue cloak billowing out behind him.

"There is treachery around, and no mistake," Caelia said as they continued walking. "Those druids…" She tailed off.

Donnell stared down at her. "How did you know I had spoken to the druids?"

She paused, looking at him. "No, I was unaware of that. My people believe that there are changes happening. For the better, some of our folk say, though others disagree. What did you notice?"

"Nothing much, except that they wouldn't help me."

She appeared to think about this. "Not, in itself, very surprising. Who is in charge of them, would you say?"

"Congal, I suppose," he said, thinking back to the earlier conversation. "Although the dark-haired man, Gabrán, was very forward with his opinions, and Fenella is not afraid to speak out either."

Caelia nodded, and they walked on. Ahead the sea came into view, the trees thinned, and Donnell saw the town of Wherrycross just below where they stood, ringed by its wall of earthworks topped with logs. He realised that at this hour, and without his mount or supplies, he had little choice but to visit the town and spend the night. Tarin would get his wish after all – he would need to seek out a different steed for the journey north.

"Farewell, then, old friend. I'll look out for your horse," Caelia said. "She sounds like a fine animal. And I'm still annoyed with you."

Without a further word, the mysterious forest woman swung herself atop a branch, and disappeared back into the trees.

* * *

The gates were closed. Donnell considered climbing them, an option that wouldn't have been open to him had he not, through circumstances, arrived on foot. It was late, but there would surely be an inn open at this time. He could bed down in the taproom and perhaps buy himself something to eat and drink. At least, he certainly hoped so – he'd had nothing but water since the hospitality of Wallace's farm in the morning, and now his trail supplies were lost, too.

The gate into Wherrycross lay on the eastern side of the town close to the Laird's Road, and during his walk there from the forest's edge, Donnell had a chance to fully check his clothing and possessions. He was relieved that the boggles had apparently not got around to searching him thoroughly – the precious note from the Laird was still folded inside his jerkin pocket. His belt pouch was missing, together with the remaining silver groats of his payment from Macswain, but a couple of silvers which he always kept secreted into the inside of his jerkin had also remained undiscovered, as had the pair of coins that he kept inside the heel of each boot, and the three that he had sewn into his belt itself, in between the two layers of leather. All in all, he would have plenty with which to pay for a night at the inn.

Getting a replacement steed was considerably beyond his means, however. He had little option but to approach Macswain for help – although he was pushing his luck in that regard, he realised, given how long he had tarried already. Hopefully the Norse threat would be seen as a mitigating factor for the delay.

Donnell was taking a small jump up, considering whether he could reasonably leap and grab a handhold on the top of the huge doors, when a face appeared above him – round and beardless, with close-set curly red hair. He stood back, wincing at the pain in his shoulders and back from his recent forest encounter, and greeted the stranger. "Well met, brother. I bring important news from Cardhu."

"At this hour? We didn't call for news. It looks more like you are a thief, seeking to burgle the homes of the good folk of Wherrycross," said the man. "Or some kind of vagabond at best." Donnell could see enough of the man to recognise that he was holding an unsheathed sword. A second guard joined him, and both looked down from the vantage point behind the top of the gates. The partner was much thinner and bonier of face, and wore a black leather helmet from which long blonde hair hung down below his scraggy beard.

"I must apologise that I was considering climbing over, good fellows. I understand how it must look. But perhaps you will understand when I tell you that I have been on the road for most of the day, and my horse has bolted when I was attacked and robbed. I simply assumed that all of the guards would be asleep."

"Asleep?" the second guard sounded genuinely annoyed now. "Are you suggesting that the Laird's men sleep through their duties? Unlike you Cardhu villagers, we are not a bunch of lazy peat cutters and turnip farmers. We are, well… we are warriors."

"Well, aye, of course. I'm so sorry, my good brave guardsmen, if I caused any offence. My name is Donnell, and I have an important message from the Laird to take to his brother in the north. But first, I…"

"A message for the Laird's brother in the north?" the first man called down, his voice raising in pitch. "It does appear that you have gone in the wrong direction, villager. Is your mind feeble, or did you get lost and turned around in the dark?"

"I am, that is to say, I have to inform his lordship of a Norse attack. My good friend Malcolm and I were down at Weir, and…"

Both heads disappeared behind the gate before he could recount any more of the morning's deadly events, and Donnell stood there for many moments, wondering if he had missed his chance for a bed for the night. It was not impossible to walk back up the coast to home, but it would take several hours, and he would be chilled through by the time he reached there.

And that was before accounting for the new Norse encampment on the coast.

The Guardhouse

As Donnell was starting to think that the conversation was over and had begun to turn away from the town of Wherrycross, the great wooden gates gave out a long creak, and began to open. Within he saw the same two guards, each struggling with a thick rope which they were using to control the movement of one of the gates.

"Come on then," called the first. Both men seemed surprisingly small, now that he saw them with their feet on the ground, and each was lightly armoured in stiff studded leather, over which they wore yellow cloaks. "Let's hear your excuses and get this gate closed up again. There are boggles around at this late hour – disgusting creatures."

"Oh, really?" said Donnell, and obliged by hurrying through the gap between the gates. The guards released the ropes, whereupon two weights dropped to the ground and the entrance slammed shut once again. The curly-haired guard moved forward and slid a wooden bar in place to hold them fast.

"Well, thanks then," said Donnell, starting to walk. "I'll be off to the inn." But the blond guard unsheathed his sword again, and quickly held it up to Donnell's chest. "I do remember, villager, that we asked you to explain yourself," he said, pointing off to the side with his other hand. "Get yourself inside there."

The first guard had finished with securing the gates, and walked over to one of the two square stone towers that flanked them on either side. He opened a door at the base of this tower, and gestured with his own sword. They were taking no chances with an unarmed man, Donnell reflected. He also noticed that their swords were beaten and rusted-looking, suggesting that they were either very old or appallingly maintained.

He stepped through the doorway of the side tower. Inside, two candles in sconces lit the square room. It was simply furnished – a bench on either side, a couple of small barrels in one corner. Two spears were also leaning against a wall, each looking as roughly treated as the guardsmen's swords.

There was a trapdoor directly in the centre of the room, too, a wooden opening about half the size of the main doorway into the tower. One of the guards picked up a candle and went to raise it. He squatted and pulled the trapdoor up, turned it right back on itself so that it was fully open, and then stood and looked at Donnell. "In there," he said. "That's your inn for the night."

"What? But what happened to questioning me?"

Donnell felt the sword point at the small of his back, and was not keen to risk another minor injury to add to his collection. He considered attempting bribery for a moment, then raised his hands and walked forwards. "All right. Keep calm, friends," he said. He crouched down at the edge of the trapdoor, let his legs down over the edge, and peered down, but could see very little in the gloom. At that point, he felt a firm kick in his lower back.

* * *

His eyes opened slowly.

Light was streaming in from a crack high on one of the walls, showing that morning had broken. Before dropping off to sleep in the dark the evening before, Donnell had felt his way around the small enclosure. It was too high for him to reach up to the trapdoor, that was clear, though not so high that the fall had done him much damage, in part due to landing on all fours on a heap of rough sacking material.

There were no windows or doors in the cellar – it was a very simple square dungeon room. He had assumed himself to be alone, and had settled down to sleep quite quickly despite his hunger, assuming that the morning would be the right time to sort out any misunderstandings.

However, although it was still very murky, the light arcing inwards now provided enough illumination to see his surroundings fully – and to see that he had company. A small, cloaked, child-like figure was curled in the far corner. Donnell sat up, and got to his feet, feeling aches in every part of his body. "Hello there, young one," he said. There was no response.

He stepped across the uneven earthen floor of the cell, and prodded at the figure. Again, there was no movement, and it crossed his mind that perhaps his cellmate was dead. And immediately afterwards, he wondered if the same fate would befall him – how long were they planning to keep him here for?

Tentatively, he reached out, and lifted the front of the figure's cloak hood with one finger, at which point its owner suddenly stirred. Donnell started, and stepped backwards abruptly. As the creature sat up and pulled back its hood, he saw the familiar look shared by his many tormentors of the day before – wide, wicked eyes with a dull glow to them, and long flat ears. Unless his mind was playing tricks, it was another boggle.

"We meet again," said the creature, in its slightly rasping, undulating voice, which Donnell found more than a little unnerving. It stood up, and on seeing it standing in its cloak, Donnell recalled the encounter that he and Caelia had had on their way out of Holm's Wood.

"The spy?" he asked. Now he clearly recognised that it was indeed the same blue cloak, which had been hard to make out in the gloom. He noted also that the creature's eyes were more of a purplish shade than the usual red of its kind.

"Well, you're a charmer, aren't you," the creature replied. "Yes. We meet again." Pulling its cloak more tightly around its body, it walked over to the source of the light. He was only a little taller than Caelia – perhaps four feet, or four and a half – and stood considerably below the level of the chink in the brickwork.

"Apologies. I was just remembering that conversation in the woods, and I've only just woken up, and not yet recovered my manners. Although of course, I could be right – here you are following me again, it seems."

"You humans are really not very bright, are you? If you recall, I was ahead of you on the path to Wherrycross. I got here first, too, and so it is you who appears to have followed me."

Donnell cleared his throat. "Well, I didn't really mean any offence." He suddenly wondered at himself, apologising repeatedly to a boggle – a creature typically considered somewhere between vermin and criminal, with the worst aspects of both.

"We'd better escape, you know," said the boggle. "Indeed, I suppose I owe you some thanks for waking me. My kind don't tend to rise at this hour." He looked all around at the dingy cell. "It's a pity my master isn't here," he added. "He's rather good at finding himself on the correct side of walls."

"Well, let's see if we can find a weak spot."

"Yes. And we'd best hurry, too. Soon after sunup they will come to take us to the Laird's Hall for entertainment."

"That sounds… nice."

The creature looked around, narrowing its purple eyes even further, then returned its gaze to the light source. "For them, perhaps. I hope you don't think that the townsfolk put the likes of me in here for my safety or comfort. They like to collect specimens to amuse the warriors for combat sports. I'll be given something like a spade, and assigned to hand-to-hand combat with some drunken warrior who is twice my size and holding a spear or an axe, while his comrades laugh and drink ale."

"I'm sorry," Donnell said, and again wondered at what he was saying.

"Yes. If I'm lucky, I may have to fight with the Laird's bastard son, the one they name Mac Rath. He's a real monster by all accounts, and has a full suit of iron armour like the knights of old. And in the unlikely event that a prisoner wins, they will be taken to face the King's justice, which means being mocked for a while and then hung. Oh, and the King's court is arriving today."

"Hmm. That's a rotten harvest for you. I'll speak up against it if I can."

This time, the creature turned right around, his little hands clenching onto the hems of its cloak. "For me?" He spluttered. "I don't think you quite understand the situation, forest man. We're both here for their sport."

Donnell pondered this for a moment, then held his hand down towards the small creature. "My name is Donnell. Do you shake hands? Or something else? What's your name?"

The creature gave an impish laugh, which served only to remind Donnell of his tormentors of the day before, causing him to scowl, but then it took on a more serious expression. It grabbed hold of his fingertips, giving them a single tug, and then released them. "I'm aware of the custom, Donnell. Well met. I am called Bib. And I am not what you think. I'm in service to one of your kind, and I do not engage in thieving or tormenting. Well, perhaps a little thieving, but only if there's a very good reason for it. My own kind hate me, as you might imagine."

Just then they heard the noise of footsteps up above, followed by a scraping sound, as if a bench or a barrel were being pulled across the floor.

"Quick, lift me up," Bib hissed at him, "to that gap in the wall."

* * *

Donnell helped the small creature up onto his shoulders, and then stepped up to the wall which, he realised, must face westwards towards the town itself. If they could find a way through here they would be out, yes, but would be fugitives inside the town.

Standing up on his shoulders, Bib worked at one of the large rectangular stones from which the tower was constructed, and there were crunching noises as the stone started to shift. Donnell looked up to gauge his new companion's progress, only to get an eyeful of sand and debris. The little boggle seemed to have very good balance, standing on his shoulders with no difficulty, and he was reminded of how its kindred had been able to move swiftly through the tree branches the day before.

There was another scraping noise from the floor above, and this time the trapdoor rattled, as if something had been moved from the top of it. A bolt was drawn back, and light flooded in as the door was lifted up. The round-faced guard from the night before bobbed his head down to look around.

"Got it," muttered Bib, and there was a thump as the stone came loose completely, and fell to the ground near his feet. Donnell felt Bib leap from his shoulders; the small creature was clearly narrow enough to squeeze through the opening that had been created; as he looked up, he saw its legs struggle for a moment and then disappear.

He presumed that would be the last he'd see of the spy – and a human wouldn't come close to following through the gap.

"Hoy," shouted the guard. "What's going on?" The head dipped down further as he tried to look around.

Donnell stooped and picked up the loose brick with one hand, and then walked over towards the trapdoor with it held behind his back. "Look down there, good man," he said, pointing at the corner where Bib had been sleeping. "The little boggle thief has left a pile of silver." The man momentarily looked around, whereupon Donnell jumped up and whacked him firmly on the back of the head with the brick. Round-face slumped down, teetered on the edge of the trapdoor, then collapsed like a sack of turnips onto the sacking, just as Donnell himself had fallen the night before.

"Ouch," muttered Donnell. At that point, another face peered down, and Donnell raised the rock again, but this time he saw Bib's grinning features.

"Good work, human – perhaps you're not so slow after all. And look what they usefully left beside their big gates." The little creature let down one of the heavy lengths of rope, then popped his head down again. "Don't worry – I tied it to the door, so it should take your weight." Donnell tugged at it a couple of times, and then started to clamber up.

Up in the guardroom, the blond guard was also lying unconscious – cudgelled by Bib, it appeared. The boggle picked up the guard's sword, scabbard and all, and strapped it round his shoulders. Donnell noticed that he left the man's money pouch behind.

Looking behind him at the trapdoor, Donnell realised that he had missed his chance to similarly arm himself – he didn't fancy climbing back down to see round-face and try to take the man's sword. However, looking round, he saw that the pair of spears were still leaning up against the wall, and he grabbed one of them. "Right, let's go," he said.

Bib was already peeking out of the gatehouse door, which was open just a crack. "Dung," he muttered. "It looks like we should have been just a little quicker."

Wherrycross Town

The little creature gently shut the door. "There's six armoured warriors outside on horseback," he said. "We can't fight them, and I'm not sure we can outrun them, either."

Donnell walked over and checked the barrels. One was half full of salt beef, but the other was empty. "Jump in," he said to his small companion, tipping the container onto its side, and pointing.

"In there? Is this a jest?"

"It is not. Come on – in you jump."

"Then what's the plan, Donnell?"

"Bib – there's no time for a meeting."

As the boggle squeezed himself in, grumbling, Donnell stood back and took a moment to fill his pockets with the beef from the other barrel.

He heard voices calling from outside and knew he'd have to hurry. Going back over to the prostrate blond guard, Donnell removed the man's leather helmet and put it on his own head. It was tight but wearable. He then donned the guardsman's yellow cloak. The spear would have to be left behind, he realised, and he leaned it quietly back against the wall.

Pulling the tower door open, Donnell made sure he was leaning right over the barrel as he pushed it slowly out into the square by the gate, the cloak covering most of him as he did so. Glancing sideways through the helmet's visor without lifting his head, he saw that the town gates were standing wide open. Mounted soldiers and several other locals were clustered around the mechanism at one side, where the rope was clearly cut in half and unusable. Some were looking at the gates, and others facing vaguely in his direction; they looked alert, but none appeared immediately warlike. He thought that perhaps he heard one calling over to him – he sincerely hoped not.

At that point, Donnell gave the barrel a firm shove, and it rolled on ahead of him, narrowly missing the corner of a wooden building opposite, and rolling down a lane. "Damnation," he called loudly, and began to jog after it, still looking down towards the ground and holding the yellow cloak as closely around his body as he could manage. He half expected to hear hooves on stone or feel a spear point in his back, but nobody intervened or called out as he hurried after the apparently wayward container. Rounding the corner, he broke into a sprint.

The boggle was already up and out of the barrel and making haste up ahead of him, with the barrel abandoned off to one side of the lane. Donnell followed close behind as his companion slipped this way and that, keeping his own blue hood held high around his face. This reminded Donnell to lose his own disguise; he quickly discarded the cloak and helmet at the side of the lane, confident that he was safer without them – he didn't want to have to explain where he'd got them, especially after the assaulted guards had been found. Besides, nobody around the town was likely to look twice at him while he was wearing his muddied travel clothes.

Bib signalled him to follow down another side alley, and he hurried on. They seemed to be heading downhill, towards the port. Donnell drew up beside his companion as they both slowed to a walk, and turned into a wider street. It was fully morning now, the weather only slightly overcast, and many people were up and about their business. The harbour was further down the street ahead, and he realised that they had moved more or less in a circle, coming back to a major street which – further up – connected directly to the town gate. A gate that was too far away to be seen at this point, fortunately.

Like the rest of the town, the harbour entrance was protected by earthworks and a wall of wooden logs. A further stone tower stood guarding the road where cargo was brought in. A great number of seagulls were circling and crying out.

"Are you planning to jump on a boat?" Donnell asked.

Bib shook his head, clapping his hands together gently, but didn't look up. "I know a place to hide, and a way out of the town which you may use, if you wish. I don't require gates. I told you, my master has ways of being on the correct side of a wall. And as you might have noticed, it is none too safe for me to be seen by the local guardsmen."

Donnell nodded. "But they caught you at the gates last night," he thought aloud.

Bib nodded with a slight smile. "After fleeing you and your demonic friend in the wood, I had to round the town walls, and I ran into one of the Laird's patrols. That's why I got handed over."

"Caelia means no harm," Donnell protested. "She's certainly no demon."

"Well," replied Bib, "she is what she is."

* * *

They carried on in silence. Ahead, close to where the wall met the harbour, a series of narrow, tall houses backed up against the town wall on its south face, with just an arm span of distance between each one. Bib gestured in the direction of one of these, a plaster-covered wooden construction with walls the colour of smoke and a surprisingly steeply pitched roof, giving it the appearance of a small tower. The home must have at least one loft, Donnell thought to himself.

Just then, a firm hand fell on Donnell's shoulder. He looked up, and saw the weathered face of the Laird's chief hunter, Macswain, who had given him his instructions in Cardhu just the day before.

Macswain leaned close, her hand still clamped on him. "What are you doing here, Donnell?" she said in a low, urgent voice. "If I'm not mistaken, you are in my pay to take a message to the Laird's brother. I think it was clear that you were not to run your own errands beforehand. This is urgent."

"Aye, my apologies," said Donnell, thinking fast. "It's fine to see you, Huntsmaster – I was thinking of coming to look for you. I am here because I had an issue with a horse."

"With a horse? There are plenty of horses – why travel half a day in the wrong direction?"

"Right, right," Donnell said, glancing around. Bib seemed to have made himself scarce. "That was indeed my intention, to make my way on my own mount. But I was unfortunately attacked on the road, and my beautiful mare bolted. I need to gain another mount, but there is no chance of getting another from Cardhu, for they need theirs for the harvest, and the farmer Tarin already opposed me."

Macswain released her grip and stared at Donnell with narrowed eyes, scratching at her leathery face. "If you leave now, you'll be a day late. The king arrives today to hold court, and the Laird needs his brother here soon to vote on clan succession. It's… well, never mind. Just get that message over. Come, I'll take you up to the gatehouse. There is a grey pony stabled there that you can use, though she has a foul temper and stinks like a swine. I'm giving you two groats less, mind, for this favour, and taking off another silver for the lateness. That's seven at the end, instead of ten."

Donnell looked around; he spotted Bib at the window of the smoky grey house, peering out at them. He wanted to rejoin the creature and find his safe way out, but trying further delaying tactics didn't seem to be an option now. He turned and started walking with Macswain back in the direction of the town gates, the huntswoman striking up a swift pace.

"Where were you heading to, anyway?" asked Macswain, after a couple of minutes of striding back uphill.

"Oh," said Donnell. "Actually, I was just about to relieve myself by the harbour. My bladder's full to bursting. Perhaps I should go back there and catch you up."

Macswain snorted and kept walking. "That's a strange place to do it. You can use the latrines outside of the gates, where the crofters go. Or just piss on the beach somewhere. We can't have any more time-wasting."

"Mmm… good point." They walked on, the towers of the gate coming into view ahead. "You know," Donnell added, stopping, "I really have to go. I'll drop my breeches in the alley over there, and catch you up at the gates. Do you think you could get that pony ready and onto the road in front of the gates?"

Macswain glared, fists clenching, and he was sure she was going to refuse – perhaps even strike him – but then she relented. "Fine. It's lucky you're an old apprentice of mine, or I swear, I'd kill you. I will get the pony ready. Go on, run."

For the second time, Donnell found himself scurrying through the back alleys, and making for the harbourside. He said a prayer to Cailleach Bheur that the little boggle would still be there when he arrived.

* * *

The boggle hadn't disappointed with his promised route out of the town. He had initially led Donnell into a very well-appointed house – one that could only be the residence of a minor noble, Donnell thought.

Bib had lent him a fine silver-and-white travel cloak, human sized, which he promised would keep the guards from spotting him. The creature had then shown him a secret passage that ran from the cellar of the house downwards, and apparently right under the city walls themselves.

Bib had also apparently changed his mind about hiding out in the dwelling. He, too, had taken the passage, mumbling something about new instructions from his master. Donnell found that baffling, given that they hadn't seen the master at all – and the boggle was still refusing to respond to any questioning about who he worked for, or whose house it was.

They were now to the south of Wherrycross, close to the coast. Together they made their way across the Laird's Road as it approached the gates, and walked warily northwards on its far side. They quickly realized that to approach the road while staying clear of the gates they would have to walk across the small fields of a croft; when they proceeded to do so, they heard angry protests from the crofter and his son who were tending their freshly planted land. At first, it looked like an awkward confrontation might develop – the last thing Donnell needed was to draw further attention to himself. But then, something happened that caught all of their attention.

The King arrived. Arthgal of Dumbarton, son of Dyfnwal, ruler of all the clans, the great King, overlord of the Laird of Wherrycross and Cunningham, and rightful ruler of all of the lands of Ystrad Clud, including most of Ireland too. With him came a large train of warriors and servants on horseback, having presumably – Donnell reasoned – ridden in from the Ayr valley far to the south.

The King himself rode near the front of the arriving column, flanked by two powerful armoured warriors. He was extremely fat and pink of face, and dressed in the lightest of armour. The warrior on the near side was a tall, strong-looking black-haired man, youthful of face, while the one on the far side had blazing red hair. Both wore leather armour sewn with heavy iron rings, and carried ancient-looking bronze shields. The shields were intricately carved with motifs of the gods and of the King's royal family – the hereditary rulers of all of Ystrad Clud.

It was a realm that had kept the old faith alive for centuries, but times had changed; today more and more of the lords were building shrines to the one god of the Irish. The family still claimed rulership of all of the lands of the Old North, with the exception of the islands that had been overrun with Norse savages, the Northumbrian kingdom, and the realm of the Pictish queen on the eastern coast.

The Wyvern

T he royal group turned towards the town and proceeded through the open gates, and Donnell watched as a long train of horses and wagons followed the king and his companions – ladies on ponies in fine clothes, cargoes of barrels, and further warriors with their own clan colours following on behind.

Then he felt a whack on his lower back, and realised that Bib was prompting him to move while the crofters' attention was occupied. They hurried forward, keeping a cluster of small homesteads between them and the gates to obscure the view of any sharp-eyed guardsman. Donnell looked around; wagons were still arriving, but there was no sign of Macswain or the grey pony.

"What are you hesitating for?" Bib glared at him impatiently, cutting directly towards the road and the north.

"I was expecting transport, but it looks like we'll be walking," said Donnell, following him. No doubt the chief hunter had had a change of plans, he thought, with the early arrival of the king.

But around a hundred paces on, just as the last members of the royal group were making their way in, swigging on ale as they went and looking barely fit to stay on their horses, he saw it. A grey pony had been saddled, and was tethered to a post by the edge of the road, though nobody was in sight to look after it. "She did it!" Donnell exclaimed loudly, and hurried forward.

Macswain had not been wrong about the pony. It bit Donnell twice as he was untying it in his haste to get moving, and seemed very unnerved by Bib, at whom it aimed a kick. It took all of Donnell's experience to calm the creature enough for him to swing up into the saddle, after which it became slightly easier to handle. Bib managed to mount up in front of him, again showing tremendous agility and balance as he used the post by the side of the road to swing around and then leap up into position. Donnell hadn't fully considered what Bib might plan to do next, but he accepted this without further comment.

They passed local crofters and merchants on their way towards Wherrycross. After that, there was nobody much around. Donnell looked towards the shore, craning up to catch a glimpse of Weir village, or the Norsemen. He couldn't see much, but at least there was no smoke or other signs of conflict. A large bird, some kind of sea eagle, was circling in that general direction.

They proceeded in silence for a time, passing birch and ash trees in their springtime colours. Donnell decided to ask his companion again about the house in Wherrycross. "That can't be your house, right? Unless you collect human-sized clothes and furniture," he said. "So, who lives there? Is it this master that you mentioned? And how did you know about the tunnel?"

Bib was silent for a moment, and Donnell thought that he had ignored the question. But then the small creature spoke. "You have riddled the answer out for yourself, it seems. Not one of my kind. The human-sized acquaintance is indeed my master. I know the place and its secrets – it's a safe place for me, and one where I can go freely."

Donnell pondered this. He had never heard of a boggle apprenticed to a human before. But then, he had never conceived of working together with one himself. "What exactly are you planning to do, Bib?" He asked. "I don't want to be rude, but I'm not sure how they'd react to you back in Cardhu."

There was a slight cackle at this from within the blue hood. "Really? Well, I, on the other hand, know very well how they would view me. But in any case, my business today lies elsewhere. Our paths will diverge very soon, Donnell. And then they will no doubt cross again."

As they passed a denser clump of trees to their right – tall, dark green pines – Donnell heard hooves off to the side, and he stopped and turned. There was nobody to be seen at first… but then he spotted another familiar face from the day before. It was Caelia. And she was leading his horse, Beira.

Donnell shouted in joy, and dismounted, not stopping to tether the grey mare. He patted and kissed Beira, then checked all around her for signs of injuries. The mare was dirty, with mud smeared up her legs and across her belly, too, but she was uninjured and seemed in good health, and his saddlebags and spear were still in place, too.

"She is absolutely fine," said Caelia, waving to catch his attention. "We've had a nice chat. Perhaps you are better at looking after horses than I thought."

Donnell smiled at this, then stroked Beira's head one more time and looked up. "Thank you so much for finding her," he said, feeling himself blushing. "Here I am, thanking you again. Can I, you know, repay you in some way?"

She sucked at her cheeks and put her head on one side. "You could tell me how you became friends with the little spy," she said, then lifted and pointed her finger. "He's stealing your pony, by the way".

Donnell turned and saw that Bib was now in the saddle of the grey mare, twenty paces down the road and covering more distance quickly.

"Huh," said Caelia, and tutted with her tongue. "It looks like you lost another one. I take it back – you *are* terrible at looking after horses."

He sighed. "The pony wasn't mine to lose, either. I'd best catch up with the little creature. He didn't say what destination he had in mind, but, well…" He swung himself into Beira's saddle, and patted her once more. "See you again on –" he began, but Caelia interrupted his salutation, grabbing his wrist and pointing.

"Look," she hissed.

Up ahead, a large dark shape hung in the sky, circling lazily just off the coast. He realised that he had spotted it before, but now it was clearly far, far too large to be a bird. There was no doubt at all – this was one of the wyverns of the Argyle mountains. The creatures were little more than a myth in Donnell's mind, but the older village folk had often told that a wyvern had put every village along the coast to flame two generations back, and had devoured hundreds of innocent people before flying back north to its rocky lair. They were thought by some to now be in a magical sleep, by others to have turned to stone, and by yet others to have crossed through a magical gate and flown far away to devour Irish or Norsemen or Romans.

Regardless of whether any of those things were true, a wyvern had clearly returned.

* * *

"You can't go that way." Caelia was pulling at Beira's harness, urging Donnell to turn around.

"But I have to do something."

"Don't be crazy. Only the druids can help us now."

"They will help the forest, but they won't help us. I've already asked."

She shook her head. "We'll see. But you have to get moving. The other way! I know you are thinking of your people, but you can't help them against that monster. Come on."

"No." He gently lifted her hand from the harness, and gave it a squeeze. "Thank you, Caelia. I know you are protecting me."

"So, what will you do?"

Donnell unsheathed the spear. "I'll improvise," he said. "And when

I'm done, I'll get on with what I've actually been paid to do."

Caelia had suddenly lost her usual mischievous warmth. "I know what the wyverns can do – I've seen it first hand, before you were born. They could rip a bear apart in the time it takes you to clap your hands. They can breathe flame or acid. They can fly, walk, swim. They are unstoppable." She looked pale and somewhat older than before. "Only the old magic of the druids can help us," she added, "or the gods themselves."

"Then let's pray for their help," Donnell said, and with a nod he turned the horse, and set out at a gallop.

As he rode, the menacing shape of the wyvern still hung in the sky over the sea ahead, circling high above, as if looking for a target. It could be that it just wanted to catch some fish, or a perhaps a seal, he told himself. Or then again, maybe not. An exposed horse on the beach would make a tempting morsel for the creature – he would have to be ready to dart for cover.

Despite this threat, Donnell felt good to be on Beira's back again, feeling her muscles straining as he rode. Riding fast seemed like progress after the multiple frustrations of the past day. It was cold, though, and a thin rain had begun to fall, hitting him in the face as they galloped on, with the sun cutting through high in the sky behind him as it approached its zenith.

A half mile on, he slowed to a canter, preserving his mount's energy. His hair was getting soaked, and he pulled the hood of the borrowed travelling cloak forward, noticing that the rest of him was staying nicely dry. The cloak certainly seemed to be made of very fine material, soft and warm, and he realised that if he clasped the garment closely around his face it stayed up, even though he was riding fast through a breeze. He pondered over its ownership. If he never saw Bib again to get the pony back, at least he could keep the cloak – not a fair trade from his side, perhaps, for he would have to compensate Macswain with hard silver, but better than nothing.

Looking over his shoulder back towards Wherrycross, Caelia was now nowhere in sight, but a half dozen riders had appeared on the road behind him, spear tips glinting. They were a long way back, but were moving quickly. Had they seen the Wyvern? Or heard of the Norsemen threat? Perhaps. But it was just as likely that they had heard of a fugitive from Cardhu, a villain who had knocked out one of the town guardsmen, and was consorting with evil non-humans.

Now, though, Donnell was on routes that he knew like a crofter knows his own field. Barely slowing his pace, he guided Beira over a low grassy rise, and then down onto the sandy beach. Galloping over the firm sand would allow him to make better time than the Laird's warriors, while shielding him from their prying eyes.

The wyvern had circled further away now, and come to a rest on a rocky skerry, a fair mile out from the shore. Its wings rippled, and dozens of seagulls flew up and away.

Even from this distance, Donnell's heart filled with dread as he gazed at the wyvern. This was a creature which could kill with ease and for pleasure. It could burn the houses of Cardhu, and eat villagers by the dozen. And there was next to nothing he could do against it with his simple spear.

Despite the warmth of the day, there was now a chill deep within him.

Sahar

The small fishing village of Weir sat on rocky land, and as he approached to within a few hundred paces, Donnell could make out the low cluster of houses and the ancient ruined fort that sat upon the flat rocks up ahead. He could also see what looked like the aftermath of a struggle on the beach between there and where he stood – or one that was still ongoing.

One Norse ship lay on the shore, smouldering. It had been pulled high above the waterline and secured to rocks and it was largely intact, but the smoke was rising from somewhere within its hull, and a couple of wooden boards had been knocked out of its sides with who-knows-what weapon.

A short figure with dark curly hair was standing on its prow, and a group of other figures were ranged around the vessel as well. Two further Norse longships, one very large and one smaller, a twin of the one on the beach, were approaching from out to sea, both advancing rapidly under the power of oars as well as sail.

Slowing his approach, Donnell loosed his spear from where it was stowed beneath the saddle, and readied it. Norse raiders were unlikely to let him pass unmolested.

As he approached where the ship lay, tilted slightly to one side where it had crunched into the yielding golden sand, he looked up at the curly-haired figure standing on the ship's prow, and could see that it was a woman – or an older girl, at least. She was athletically proportioned, the skin of her face as dark as a hazelnut, and was holding a crossbow, the spring-loaded weapon that Northumbrians were known to favour. She was dressed in light travelling sealskin clothes, and Donnell noticed a bloodstain on her back. And she was pointing the weapon at a group of men on the beach.

He pulled up his horse a few dozen paces short of the confrontation. At first he had taken the group of men to be Norse raiders, but on a closer look, most or all of them appeared to be villagers – people that Malcolm would know, and who the folk of Cardhu held in low regard. Uncultured and overly focused on their boats, the fisherfolk could be aggressive and easily provoked, and this group was unusually well armed, many of them holding Norse-style spears or axes. A few were even wearing helmets.

Over by the longboat, one of the villagers decided to make a move. He lunged towards the girl from down below her, close to the hull of the ship, and aimed his spear towards her legs. She spotted him at the last moment and jumped straight upwards, raising her knees close to her body, and the spear narrowly missed her calf. She whirled round, and raised the crossbow as the man lunged again, but this time his movement was cut off mid thrust, and he fell with a crossbow bolt in his shoulder, screaming, blood spattering over the sand. There was a moment's silence and then everyone was talking or shouting at once, all eyes on the girl and the damaged ship.

* * *

Donnell spurred Beira over, lowering his spear again in order to try to look less threatening, and began yelling until he got their attention. "Men of Weir, you know me. I am Donnell of Cardhu, a friend to the newcomer to your village, Malcolm. Why are you attacking this girl?

It discredits your families."

There was some muttering, and then a man who Donnell recognised as one of Alna's cousins spoke up. "Aye, we know you, Donnell. We have been tasked to protect the Norseman's boat, and this she-devil sneaked in and set fire to it." Donnell thought the man was called Lud, though he wasn't sure, for the cousins all looked rather similar to his mind. The man had muscular hairy arms and wore a smock, as did most of the villagers, and his eyes were very closely set. He had somehow obtained a battleaxe, but looked uneasy about how to wield it – the blade was pointing towards his own chest.

Two of the villagers were nursing their fallen comrade, and Donnell nudged his horse closer until he was in between Lud and the prow of the boat. "That hardly seems a reason to stick a spear through the girl," Donnell said, although he was quite sure that the fisherfolk considered any damage to boats to be a serious matter. "She's little more than a child. Perhaps I can take her to the Laird's Luftenand in Cardhu, to receive a fair hearing and the King's justice."

"The Norsemen's leader wants her. She was his prisoner," Lud replied.

"No, she wasn't," said another.

"I think she was."

After some further discussion, Lud added, "She is their escaped prisoner, we think, and certainly a dangerous and ungodly person."

"The Norsemen's affairs are of no importance to our folk," said Donnell. "Do we collect their prisoners and slaves for them, now?"

There was some further muttering, but no immediate response.

Donnell looked up at the young woman, who was staring at him suspiciously. "Can you understand my tongue?" he asked. "I am neutral here, I don't live in this village and I don't know the Norse people either. I am Donnell of Cardhu, a small town which lies in the hills up behind us. You have no reason to trust me, I understand, but I am a man of my word. Have they harmed you, and can I offer protection?"

She looked down. "They want to kill me, horse rider," she said in the Celtic language, speaking it flawlessly. "These foolish villagers trust Iohric the Ganger's men, but they shouldn't. He's a thief and a murderer. My people exiled him for his crimes."

The fishermen who had been tending to their fallen comrade got up, and looked ready to have another try at spearing the girl to end the standoff. Donnell looked up again. "Jump on to the horse, young stranger, and I will take you to safety. This could get bloody for both of us if we stay here."

He nudged Beira closer again to the boat's prow, glaring down at the villagers, and pointed his spear in their direction. "Back off!" he shouted. Two of them instead turned to him, approaching with spears in their hands. At that moment, he felt the woman had leaped onto the back of Beira behind him. The man Lud was still standing there stupidly, fiddling with his axe, but the closest pair lunged.

Donnell spurred Beira forward, but didn't have time to build up any momentum. He turned in his saddle, deflecting one spear with his own, and ducking under the point of the other. He heard a click as the woman loaded her crossbow again, and he aimed a kick at the closest man, who recoiled, dropping his spear and clutching at his nose.

The other spearman lunged again, but this time Donnell parried the move and struck back, his own spearpoint slicing past the man's face and opening a gash on his cheek. But by now Beira was cantering, moving them quickly away from the scene and out of danger.

Most of the other villagers stood back out of the way of the accelerating horse, but one heavy-set black-bearded man walked into their path, weaving a battle axe in a figure-of-eight pattern in front of him. This was no villager but a Norse warrior among their ranks. Donnell continued his approach and then swerved to one side at the last moment, lashing out with the butt of his spear. He caught the man full on the forehead, and didn't wait to see how he recovered, instead guiding

Beira up and across the dry sand at the top of the beach.

After a few moments they were making their way across the rough grass of the sand dunes and out of sight.

* * *

They galloped along the road that led to Weir village, Donnell intending to turn up the main track towards Cardhu itself. He remembered his friend Malcolm's words – *first they made camp by the shore, a mile up the coast from Weir*. That meant northwards, he was sure, meaning that he should be able to reach the major path that connected Cardhu and Weir before reaching the main Norse camp. Unless the heathens were now camped out on the Laird's Road itself, he reflected.

The Norsemen must now be in control of the local people, at least to an extent – that was apparent from the way the local men were doing the invaders' bidding on the beach, and was no doubt a direct result of the arrival of warriors that he had recently witnessed. They must have occupied Weir and made servants or slaves of the locals. Well – at least the village folk had not simply been slaughtered, as he and Malcolm had first feared.

When he felt that they were far enough ahead of their foes on the beach, Donnell slowed to a trot, and secured his spear below the saddle once again. He was keen to preserve Beira's energy; she had already worked hard, had not enjoyed a proper stable for the night, and now had two passengers to carry. "Are you all right?" he asked, half turning. "You're wounded, I think?"

"I'm fine," the young woman answered. "The blood is from an older wound, several days back."

"Right."

He looked back up the road in the direction from which he had come, and could still see the spear points of the mounted warriors from

Wherrycross, but only just. Those men were a fair distance back – they must have stopped for a time, or otherwise been delayed. Out to sea, he could see the dark shape of the wyvern still perched on the skerry, and although it had hunkered down and appeared to be resting, a chill ran though him again at the sight of the deadly beast.

Weir village itself lay ahead, only a few hundred paces away.

"Threats in every direction," he muttered.

He glanced again back over his shoulder at the young woman, whose expression had barely changed. "What do you know of the Norse people at Weir village," he asked. "They are your people, aye? And do they mean to invade this kingdom?"

She was silent for a moment, then said, "I was their prisoner, on the great longship – the one that is out to sea over there." She pointed. The two ships appeared to be midway between the coast and the Isle of Arran, though it was hard to judge, and one was double the size of the other.

"Four ships arrived," she continued, "but most of their people are further up the coast, building a wooden stronghold and raiding small homesteads to gather food. Those two ships returned to Iohric's own castle to pick up more warriors and supplies. His strength is growing and his forces will strike when they are ready. You can't trust those people, so do not attempt to treat with them. They will tell you one lie after another."

"Those people? Are you not from their lands?"

"My name is Sahar al-Rahman. I am of Córdoba, and was taken as a child by the greatest warrior of the north islands, Hrólfr the Red. You have probably heard some of the stories of his bravery and exploits? He has lain waste to whole towns within a morning, and burned hundreds of enemy ships to the waterline."

"I see."

"I tell you, he is a true hero, and it is not for nothing that he exiled the white-haired warrior, Iohric. Your people are in great danger from Iohric, not that those fools on the beach would listen. This is his method – he treats with the locals until he has established a fort and moved more warriors into position, and then he slaughters any that he can't use as slaves."

"So, they are working with the villagers right now?"

Sahar paused, and then sighed. "I think so. Most of those fishermen seem to be helping, and Iohric's men have equipped them with stolen weapons from fallen warriors – another crime, for the slain men should be buried with their weapons."

Donnell pondered this for a moment. The last he had seen of Malcolm, he was going to warn the locals and encourage Alna and her kinsfolk to flee – it didn't seem like the mission had been a success. Had his friend got out safely, and where was he now? He would have to to his best to find out – and he had now taken on the responsibility to somehow get young Sahar to safety, too.

It was now beginning to dawn on Donnell that he was not going to be able to make it to Inverkip with the Laird's message that day – and perhaps not at all. Failing to do so, of course, meant giving up on the opportunity offered to him by Macswain. His chance of freedom.

But what good was freedom if his village was threatened by a murderous wyvern, and the kingdom itself was in peril from invading Norsemen?

No.

The Laird may understand the circumstances, or he may not. In truth, the nobleman was known for being a petty drunkard, and Donnell had already broken at least a couple of laws in his escape from Wherrycross. Further displeasure from failing to deliver the note could result in his becoming much better acquainted with the inside of a prison cell.

Or worse.

But all the same, it was becoming clear to Donnell what he had to do. His companions and his village were under threat, and both the Norse and the wyvern were threatening Cardhu. And the druids were not coming to their aid.

Just then, he heard shouts from further down the road. Despite the much greater threats that were closing in on the village, his immediate priority had to be to get away from the thugs from the beach.

Donnell spurred Beira on.

At the Crossroads

Up ahead was a thick stand of trees where there had once been a croft, but one that had always tended to be waterlogged, and had been abandoned a generation back. "Here," Donnell said. "Quickly. We can stay out of sight until they pass."

They dismounted and moved into the trees, leading Beira, and quickly making themselves well concealed from the road. Most of the trees had only small spring leaves and buds, but there were large whin bushes among the ruined walls of the tumbledown building, and between these and the walls themselves, there was plenty of cover. He led Beira round to the back of the building and stopped. Now he just needed to hope that the horse would keep quiet.

Donnell then took a moment to catch his breath, and looked at Sahar properly for the first time. She couldn't have seen more than fifteen or sixteen summers, but was muscular and tough-looking, with many scars upon both arms. Her eyes were black, as was her long curly hair. "Look, we need to get to my home, Cardhu, up beyond the hills. We'll be safe there, or at least *safer*, and can plan our next move. But there are too many dangers on this road right now."

Even as he said the word 'danger', a vision of the wyvern filled Donnell's mind again, and a familiar chill passed through him as his eyes flitted out towards the coast. But the beast was now out of sight from where they were.

Gritting his teeth, he tried his best not to think about it, and he looked at Sahar again. "You think you can wait here quietly until we find a good time to move?"

She nodded tersely. "Donnell, is it?"

"That's right. And you are Sahar?"

She nodded.

He tied Beira's harness lightly to a birch sapling. Nearby, a trickling burn ran down between a gap in a drystone wall further back, crossed the area, and then disappeared into a culvert under the road itself. The horse dipped her head to drink, after which Donnell started to feed her handfuls of oats from the saddlebags, patting and rubbing her sweating sides gently.

"Is there time to see to the horse?" asked Sahar.

He glance around at her. "Habits from my old training as a woodsman, I suppose. A stop would often be an opportunity to see to the animals, especially when they have been worked hard."

Sahar stepped forward and stroked the horse's nose. "Such a beautiful animal." She then turned and crept forward past the main ruined building and back towards the road, crouching low and looking carefully to both sides. The approaching travellers sounded very close now, and Donnell wondered if she was being careless – or could she actually be planning to betray him?

Leaving Beira tethered, he moved forward after her and peered around from behind the trunk of a mature ash tree. He was relieved when Sahar ducked down behind a badly broken-down section of drystane wall which had once marked the front edge of the abandoned croft, gaining a vantage point from which she was still well covered. She crouched and silently readied her crossbow.

Bending low and moving as slowly and quietly as he could, Donnell came over beside her. Only a few moments had passed before they saw a group of Weir villagers mixed together will more well-armoured

Norse warriors. But rather than the ones that they had seen before, these ones were heading southwards on the road, towards the damaged ship. And as Donnell and Sahar watched on, they saw three of the fisherfolk from the beach hurrying in the direction from which they had just come. The two groups met on the road not far from where the pair were hiding, somewhat to their left.

Donnell immediately noticed that one of the Norseman on the far side of the group was a head-height taller than the average, and was clad in an ornate iron breastplate. He had long white braided hair, and carried a shield and sword. He also had an enormous battle axe strapped to his back.

Donnell looked round to catch Sahar's attention and check whether this was indeed Iohric, only to have his question answered for him – the woman had her crossbow trained on the man, and looked ready to pull the trigger.

"Psst," he said insistently, raising his hand to block her shot; she glanced round with a scowl, and then lowered the weapon. Donnell placed his hand on her arm, wondering at her reckless lack of judgement. Whatever the cause, Sahar clearly held a murderous dislike for Iohric, the Norse leader.

* * *

The group on the road spoke for a short while, but it was difficult for Donnell to make out anything that they were saying, largely because the nearest men were all Norse and were speaking loudly in their own harsh language. Donnell saw one of them point southwards on the road, and the white-haired warrior hold up his hand to look, shielding his eyes from the sun, and nodded to his immediate companions – two muscular axemen, each of them in jet-black cloaks. Donnell craned his neck to see whether the Laird's men from Wherrycross were in sight, but he was unable to see any more from their hiding place. He guessed that they had seen the spearmen and perhaps the wyvern too, and were discussing what to do next.

"What was that move?" whispered Donnell, still crouched behind the ruined wall. "You need to think before you act, Sahar. If you'd shot at him, even if you'd hit, they would all have come at us at once."

Sahar shrugged sullenly, carefully clipping the crossbow to her belt, then looked up at him with a slight smile. "It's lucky you stopped me, then," she said softly. "But I need to take that man down. I hope it is not long before I get another chance."

After a couple of minutes, Donnell risked another peek towards the road. The Norsemen were beginning to move off, having turned southwards towards the beached longship – and towards the riders. But he was unable to see Iohric among their company, and the riders were not visible from their position either.

"This is our chance – we need to get going while that group of warriors are making their way south," he said. "We'll go towards my village now, while it's clear. Dealing with Iohric can wait a while."

Sahar stood up from behind the wall, and looked in both directions. "Which way do you mean?"

"To our right," he said. "Just as we come close Weir village, we will see the main trail up towards Cardhu. I think we can hurry past and make our way up that trail and out of sight of enemies."

They waited for another couple of minutes to be sure, and then proceeded out onto the road, leading Beira by the harness, and sticking to the grassy verge to minimise the noise of her hooves. Turning northward, they hurried towards the crossroads.

"What am I thinking," said Donnell, more to himself than to Sahar. "If there are more Norsemen on the main road beside Weir itself…"

"Then let's hope they are busy being evil somewhere else."

He sighed. "Yes."

"And at least they won't know you."

He looked around. "But they are after you, if I am not mistaken. What if some of them are guarding the path, and they see you?"

She shrugged. "If they do, I'll stick a bolt through their eyes, quick. Then they won't see anything. I am quite accurate, you know."

He shook his head, smiling slightly. "I noticed."

* * *

The midday sun was high in the sky, with no further signs of rain. To their left the sea looked dark, though, where the two Norse ships were still rapidly approaching.

Donnell and Sahar continued for the few hundred paces beyond until they reached the crossroads where a wide but rough track led off uphill to Cardhu, and a smaller one still led across the rock flats down to Weir. Many trees and large bushes overhung the road in each direction.

And they paused there for a moment, Donnell saw Malcolm approaching from the opposite direction. His old friend was deep in conversation with a helmeted stranger, and neither appeared to have noticed Donnell and Sahar yet. The muscular former blacksmith was still holding his maul, but the conversation looked peaceable enough. He felt Sahar shrink back to one side of the road, but Donnell muttered, "It's fine. We can trust that one."

He walked out into the centre of the road, giving a low whistle to attract his friend's attention. Malcolm looked up, either at the whistle or the dull clicks of Beira's hooves, and nodded with a smile. "Well met," said Donnell. As he walked up to the pair, he recognised the helmeted man as Alna's brother Saul. The man was wearing Norse armour and carrying a rusted spear.

"Welcome back," his friend replied. The brother-in-law fell silent, twisting the spear in his hand as they approached.

Donnell narrowed his eyes at Saul, wary that the man may now be working for the Norse. He considered loosing his own spear from where it was stowed, but resisted the temptation to do so. "I'm afraid the druids were useless, old friend. They say they can't get involved."

Malcolm nodded slightly, blowing his cheeks out. "Well, then we can only hope for a miracle. Thank you for trying, Donnell."

"And what of Alna, is she safe?"

"She's still in Weir. She's staying with her brothers, who are now working for the Norsemen." He spoke matter-of-factly, but his eyes were red and watery, and he looked deeply troubled.

Donnell nodded. "I gathered that they have accepted the Norseman Iohric as their leader, at least for now."

"Perhaps, yes – I don't know. The locals have struck some kind of deal. I have managed to stay away from them, but for now, they appear to be safe. " Malcolm looked over Donnell's shoulder and nodded slightly in Sahar's direction. "I see you've found the fugitive," he added. "Be careful of that one – she's already put a bolt in one of Alna's cousins."

Donnell glanced back at his companion, who was holding back slightly, and was glad to see that she was keeping her crossbow pointed downwards. "She's a fierce one right enough, and a skilled archer. It didn't seem right to let the Norsemen and their lackeys stick a spear through her, so I'm taking her up to Cardhu, and then we will see what happens after."

Malcolm exchanged a look with the helmeted Saul, but didn't reply. Saul nodded his head slowly as if thinking, and then, without a word, started walking down towards Weir village, boots clacking on the huge slabs of sandstone that lined the shore at this point.

"Where's he going?" asked Sahar. The others shrugged. "I don't trust him," she said. "We should knock him out just in case."

Malcolm sighed, looking after the departing man. "I think we can forget about him. He's too stupid to plan anything harmful."

"In any case, we should get off the road, my friend," said Donnell, as his eyes also followed the man's path and then looked in either direction along the coast. "There's a huge gang of Norsemen just south of here, and a group of the Laird's knights are heading up the coast. This place could be a battleground before long."

"Then let's go home." Malcolm gestured uphill with his maul, the enormous muscles of his arm rippling. He started up the path towards Cardhu village, Donnell and Sahar following, and stopped after a few paces, moving over beside the trees at the side as the path began to curve.

"Listen, Donnell," Malcolm spoke again, his voice low. "It's risky to get involved in this." He nodded towards Sahar. "We have our own people to protect. This is a Norse dispute from what I have heard, an old family feud. Iohric's men consider the girl their property – spoils of war. And if they find you're sheltering her…"

"Best not tell them, then," Donnell replied.

"They're liars," Sahar broke in. "I'm no property of theirs. My father is Hrólfr the Red, and those men follow a black-hearted traitor."

Malcolm looked at her, his mouth open, but didn't say anything.

"She seems to know what she's talking about," Donnell added. "Besides, it must be very clear by now that the people of Weir shouldn't trust the Norse. Not only are they violent raiders and murderers, they are most likely liars, too. It's not safe to bargain with them."

"I've been telling them that." Malcolm looked down and slung his maul back into his belt as they spoke.

"It's total idiocy," said Sahar. "They'll end up slaves, or worse."

Malcolm looked at her. "How so?"

She looked him up and down. "Iohric. He's a snake. He makes deals and breaks them, forms alliances and then stabs his allies in the back."

"Go on, please."

"He will use the people to help build up a fortification. Once it is built, he will slaughter the elderly and young children, and sell the rest into slavery. It's what he does – it has happened before in other kingdoms." She wrinkled up her face, looking back up the road. "People here just don't know who they are dealing with."

"But now that we know more about what the Norse might be planning, perhaps we can tell the folk here," said Donnell, looking at them both intently. "Ask them again to flee up to Cardhu for protection."

Malcolm stroked his chin. "Look, if what you are saying is true, we need to persuade the people of Weir of the danger they are in. But we can't take this girl into Weir village to tell them – it would start a blood bath."

"I've noticed that already," Donnell nodded.

Malcolm paused. "Well then. I've said it before – they might listen to you, Donnell, even if they won't listen to me. Would you ride down with me and speak to Alna and her kin?"

Donnell looked at Sahar, who stared back at him, eyes slightly narrowed. "I'd be happy to," he said, "but I've said I will stay with her, and that's what I intend to do."

Malcolm stepped closer to his friend and lowered his voice. "You're a natural leader, Donnell – always have been. When you speak, people listen. You just need to choose to get involved for once."

Donnell suddenly felt tired, really noticing the aches of his multiple small injuries from the day before for the first time in a while. He shook his head and stepped away. "It's kind of you to say that, but I don't think it's really true."

"Donnell, if you're worried about getting the girl safely up to Cardhu, it's just at the top of this track," said Malcolm, pointing with his hammer. "She's armed and dangerous, and I will accompany her, too. None will stop us."

Donnell glanced down in the direction of the shore, and could make out the cluster of a dozen houses that made up the fishing village, with the ancient ruined fort on a small rise off to one side. All looked relatively normal – peaceful, even – with just a few plumes of smoke rising from the smokehouses. "All right," he said. "If you take the girl up to Cardhu with you, be quick, and keep a low profile. Remind her not to shoot anyone, too."

"Donnell – please make sure that this news about the Norse reaches Alna and her family," said Malcolm. "Hearing it from you might make all the difference."

Donnell nodded, and mounted Beira again, patting the horse on the neck and turning in the road as he looked down at his companions. "I will catch up with you both as soon as I can. Any suggestions about how to deal with the Norsemen if I see them?"

Malcolm looked up at his old friend. "Use your experience. Make them afraid. And if that fails – run."

The Two Ships

Beira trotted down the track under Donnell's guidance. The woodsman looked this way and that for signs of an ambush. He could see the two longships very clearly now, for they were not more than a mile out from shore. Both were traditional vessels of a type that he had seen in the past – narrow gauged, dark wooden ships with a single high rectangular sail, and notches for oars. Each had a rising wooden prow at the front, the smaller one a fish, and the larger one a magnificent carved figure of a dragon head, complete with jagged teeth. The smaller ship had edged ahead of its partner, and neither would take long before they arrived at Weir village itself, as both were being rowed as well as benefitting from a good breeze hitting their sails.

The houses were just up ahead of him now, a small cluster close together in a rough circle, with another few straggling along the shore path in either direction. Each house was very small compared to the large roundhouses and wooden shacks that most people lived in up at Cardhu. He could see abandoned fishing gear, badly tended vegetable plots and broken tools lying here and there on the path up ahead.

Further on was a tiny wooden chapel, smaller than the gatehouse that he had recently been captured in, and made entirely of wood. It, too, was badly maintained, with moss and signs of damp along the upper edge of the planks. Two roughly cut branches formed an upturned arch above the door to which a cross was attached. Nearby, four men were bringing rocks up from the shore and piling them up beside this chapel.

As Donnell approached the cluster of dwellings, three men walked out from the nearest house. He recognised the helmeted Saul who had recently left them at the crossroads; the others were an older man with a white-yellow beard and a skinny youth, each holding a sword. Further back he saw a single Norse axeman, dressed in a black cloak like the pair he had seen on the road. Unlike the villagers, this man remained where he was, leaning against the front of one of the houses, watchful. However, the four other villagers down near the chapel left their rock lifting task, and came up to join in behind Saul. There was no way past them – that was clear.

Donnell's heart was racing at the prospect of a violent confrontation with the men. He pulled up Beira, and half turned her, and then held one hand up as he took hold of his spear. "Don't attack me. Back off. I could take one of you down with my spear before you got a step closer," he called out.

The men looked at each other, and then Saul removed his helmet and spoke.

"We know you, Donnell of Cardhu, although you have come here dressed and mounted like a lord. We don't wish you any harm, but you are not welcome here any more."

Donnell kept his spear held high. "Man, you heard us talking up there by the road. The Norsemen can't be trusted – we need to come together to fight them off. They are led by a notorious criminal, and will bring death and misery to our people if we don't."

"Perhaps," said the older man. "But as my father used to say, perhaps the sea will take you tomorrow." He waved behind him. "See how their ships are coming? We can't fight them off. Our only choice is to do as they ask."

"Those men are warriors, many in number and heavy with armour," added Saul, glancing nervously at the black-cloaked warrior as he spoke. "We had no choice but to follow their instructions, and they have treated us honourably so far."

"Besides, we think we can trust them," added the elder, "at least, as well as we trust the tides and the weather, which is to say it's just another uncertainty. You should do the same, if it's not to come to a fight."

Donnell said, "This is foolish talk. These Norse folk are known raiders and slavers. You should take your people to Cardhu, as many as you can. There you can shelter in safety until we are able to gain help from the Laird to run them off the land and send them back to their ships."

The black cloaked Norseman twisted his axe in his hand, but said nothing.

"I don't think you can fight them at Cardhu, either," the old man replied. "One Luftenand and a group of farmers. Not exactly a fighting force."

"We are lucky. The king and dozens of his knights are at Wherrycross right now," replied Donnell. "We can stop them if we band together now, and get help from our rulers."

The smaller longship was almost at the shore now, and he realised that he was going to need to move quickly. The larger was still a few hundred paces out.

* * *

Donnell spoke to Saul again. "Good man, come on – listen to me. You have a clan, children to care for. We need to get them up to Cardhu where they'll be safe. The moment the Norsemen decide that they no longer need you, you'll be slaughtered, and your women and children sold into slavery. Please, don't be reckless."

The man looked stupidly forward, as if speaking to Beira. "No. You will all have to do as they say and swear on Loki's belt. Then you'll be safe."

"Loki's belt?"

"It's what they use. If you swear to their gods, you're one of their men," Saul explained. "That makes you safe."

"But… isn't that against your beliefs?" Donnell said, glancing past him towards the chapel.

"It just means loyalty," added the bearded one. "A safe refuge."

Donnell shrugged. "I hope you are right, but I fear the worst." He sighed. "Well, can I speak to Alna? I have a message for her, from Malcolm."

The men looked at each other, and there was a pause. Then the younger one said, "Alna? Nay. She swore on the belt, like her kinsmen. She left with Iohric, the Norse leader. She isn't here anymore. We don't know where she is, but she's certainly not Malcolm's betrothed now."

"That's…" Donnell began to object, but he didn't finish his sentence. At the edge of his attention, the dark shape of the wyvern had taken to the sky and was coming steadily closer, circling lower and lower. Suddenly realising how close it was, he looked up in alarm.

The scaly beast cut through the air with ease; it had two great bat-like wings and a long tail, but it certainly didn't look like a bat or bird. The shadow it cast over the sea was enormous.

As he watched it swoop along, parallel with the coast but still high above the scene, the dark shape suddenly bunched up, compressing and changing shape until it was like an arrowhead, and then started to plunge rapidly downwards towards the water. Down it went, faster and faster in a hunting dive, as he had seen falcons do in the Laird's lands when he was a youth.

And then it struck. The cracking noise took a few seconds to reach him, but he saw the larger longship crumple in the middle, its sail flap loosely like a rag and then catch fire, a hundred timbers seeming to fly in every direction. One larger piece, the rear half of the ship's hull, still floated well above the waterline, and the creature landed on it, balancing. Then it shook itself slightly, and blasted a ball of green fire which set a dozen broken pieces of timber aflame.

The wyvern flapped its wings twice and then lazily lifted off again, carrying two body-sized shapes in its jaws, and the water continued to flame behind it for many moments. A few desperate screams could be heard from where the onlookers stood.

The great creature circled once more and then flew away from shore for a few moments, before settling again on the tiny rocky skerry to devour its catch.

Having been standing still, watching in horror, the villagers now began running in every direction, entering homes and barring doors, their discussion with Donnell forgotten.

With his heart thumping and visions of his closest companions being similarly ripped apart by the wyvern filling his mind, Donnell turned Beira, and spurred her towards Cardhu.

* * *

He caught up with Malcolm and Sahar just below the village. The pair turned at the sound of his approach and Sahar raised her crossbow, but both visibly relaxed when they recognised him.

He dismounted to spare his horse; Beira had made great pace, and even though he had to slow at the steepest points, he had worked her hard on the climb, and she was breathing hard. "Did you see that?" he asked.

The pair nodded. "It was incredible," said Malcolm. "Terrifying. Surely we all have to flee – nothing could stop that."

"The villagers were running when I left. But I spoke to them, and they told me that they had struck a deal with the Norse," said Donnell. "I'm sorry – I really tried, but they wouldn't listen to me about the dangers they were putting themselves in. I'm obviously not as persuasive as you think I am."

"And Alna?"

Donnell paused, then leaned across and put a hand on Malcolm's shoulder. "I'm sorry, old friend, but she and her kin have sworn loyalty to the Norse. They said she is no longer with you."

Malcolm said nothing, but his fist clenched, his one arm rippling, and he stared at the ground in silence for a long moment. Then he cursed at the top of his voice and kicked out at a rotten tree at the side of the road, sending splinters flying across the path ahead.

Donnell caught Sahar's eye; she was looking unsettled, but said nothing. He took the opportunity to glance up into the sky behind them. He wasn't able to see the beast, which did not reassure him at all.

"They might have been lying to me, Malcolm. Who knows what plans those crab-eaters have made."

Malcolm took a couple of deep breaths, looking down at his one clenched fist as if deep in contemplation. Then he responded, "You said it yourself, Donnell. They are idiots – too stupid to lay traps for us with their words."

"That's the truth," added Sahar. She had now clipped her crossbow to her belt, and was trying a cord around her curly hair to keep it back from her face. Just then, Malcolm pointed with his hammer to the sky behind them. They all looked around to see that the wyvern had taken to the sky again, and was rising and circling at a distance. And it was now above the shore, rather than the water.

"We have to keep moving," said Donnell. "We're almost there."

The way curved round up ahead for a few hundred paces, after which, as both men knew, the first few houses of Cardhu would come into sight. But as they walked, their surroundings became less and less clear. Mist seemed to be rising in waves, as if from the ground itself. It thickened and swirled in front of their eyes until the way ahead towards home was shrouded with a deep fog.

Eochaid

onnell shook his head twice and blinked rapidly, wondering if he was feeling dizzy from the shock of what had happened down at the shore, but it made no difference. As he looked around, the surroundings continued to fade until they were standing in the thickest of fogs. He heard Sahar speaking in her own language, sounding fearful and agitated, and he slowed his pace.

Within moments, the trees and even the road were impossible to make out within a mist of solid white. He could barely make out his companions, or even Beira, whose harness he was still holding. He stopped walking completely, unsure of his footing.

Malcolm hissed, "Donnell! It is the cloaking mist, the *féth fíada*. The old sorcerer Eochaid taught me about it."

"You mean that *you* did this?" Sahar asked sternly.

"No, of course not. I can't do it myself, and I don't think Eochaid could either – he read about it in a book, and told me when I was just a lad."

"It must have been the druids," said Donnell. "It's the only explanation. They refused to help us when I spoke to them, but the appearance of the wyvern might have changed their minds."

"Aye, I suppose that makes sense," Malcolm agreed.

"So how do we get through it?" asked Sahar.

"Let's walk forward, but be careful," Malcolm replied. "The druids will be at the centre, and it will be clearer there, I'm fairly sure."

"All right," said Donnell. "Can you both feel Beira's harness or stirrups? If you hold them, I can try to lead you."

Sahar said, "Yes. Yes, I've got hold of part of it."

When Malcolm also confirmed that he was holding on to Beira's tack, Donnell took a few paces forward, stepping very carefully. The horse resisted, fearful of the strange mist, but he spoke in gentle tones, giving out a sense of reassurance that he didn't feel himself, and Beira started to walk, nuzzling her face against his arm as they went.

This road had been familiar to him almost since he first learned to walk, and he knew that he could easily pass this way and that even in the dead of night. All the same, something about the mist seemed to attack his senses. It was so absolute that it made him feel slightly nauseous, as if his vision and balance were being scrambled. As he walked on, he realised that sounds and smells were muffled too. It was deeply disconcerting – and the thought of a wyvern circling unseen in the sky, ready for another attack, didn't help at all.

They kept going forward, pace by pace. The muffling of sound must have some kind of limited range, for he could hear Beira's occasional whicker and whinny very clearly, as well as Malcolm's breathing. Sahar was quieter, but he could sense that she was still there, and every now and then he heard a curse in an unfamiliar tongue.

Donnell was quite sure that he would know how far up the road he had walked even if he did it blindfold, but again, he realised, the féth fíada was dulling this aspect of his intuition. He found himself simply putting one foot in front of the other, swapping his hand on the horse's rein so that he could feel out to both sides with a free hand, and sometimes adjusting his direction of travel when his fingertips touched against leaves or branches.

He had little sense of time, too, as they travelled through the mist. He began to regret not counting his steps, which could perhaps have allowed him to work out in his head how long it would have taken from their starting position in the village. But then, was the village entirely cloaked in mist, too, and where exactly were the druids? Would he even be able to find his home this way? How far had they come – half way? Three quarters? He kept walking, unsure of their progress or where exactly they were heading.

And then, all at once, he found himself blinking at an unexpected change, as the féth fíada was suddenly gone, or was at least more distant, and he struggled to focus on the newly visible surroundings. He found himself staring into the centre of Cardhu, itself surrounded by a vast impenetrable cloud.

Looking around, as his eyes adjusted once again to depth and distance, he could make out an almost perfect white circle around Cardhu, for the edge of the mist surrounded all of the more central houses of the village, and rose like a dome above. It seemed to circumscribe the smallest circuit round the houses possible, touching the corners of walls in some places.

On the road up ahead stood a familiar short figure in a blue cloak, alongside an old man with long white hair. Bib, cloak wrapped tight around him but with hood back, was looking over towards them, his head tilted to one side. The little boggle took a few steps towards them, smiling at Donnell and clapping his hands together quietly.

Donnell looked at his companions and saw that Sahar looked surprised and thoughtful, but Malcolm had fear and fury in his eyes. Before Donnell could think of how to explain his new connection with Bib, his friend ran forward, loosing his enormous maul and swinging the great hammer-weapon above his head with a deep growl.

* * *

As Malcolm dashed the few dozen paces towards Bib, the old man with the white hair lunged forwards onto the road and brought up a sword to parry the maul's blow, protecting Bib from any harm. Donnell expected the older man's sword to be knocked easily out of the way, but somehow he held his grip against the younger man's immense strength.

At that moment, Donnell realised that the old man was no stranger. The hand on the sword's hilt was scaled like the skin of a lizard, and he realised that he was looking at Eochaid, the old spellcaster who had lived in the wilderness nearby when he was just a child. The man's long hair half-covered his face instead of being tied back as he had seen in the past, but the cropped beard and large bulbous nose were unmistakable, as was the deformity of his hand. Was the old man somehow connected to Bib?

Not waiting for the outcome of this struggle, Bib ducked and rolled out from under the crossed weapons. The little creature stood and hurried towards Donnell and Sahar, and gave a deep bow to each of them in turn. "Well met, cell companion," he said to Donnell with a smile. "I'm glad to see you've parted ways with that tree-witch."

"Who – or what – is this?" Sahar asked, looking down and recoiling slightly from the boggle as if he had an overpowering smell that she was trying to escape from.

"Sahar, this is Bib. We have only just met, but I think he can be trusted. At the very least, he's a lot better than most of his people."

"You are too kind," said Bib, wryly.

Malcolm, too, had recognised Eochaid, and after their brief clash of weapons they had embraced, and then joined in rapid conversation.

"He's surprisingly intelligent, as well," Eochaid was saying as the pair walked over, all hostility forgotten. "He can read, and even do research for me. Of course, it can be difficult to travel with a boggle, but I can usually pass him off as a sleeping child if anyone asks. He's good at hiding himself away though, of course, so that is rarely necessary."

Malcolm nodded. He didn't look entirely convinced and still kept his distance from Bib, but at least the maul was back at his side for now.

"I see you're enjoying my cloak," said Eochaid to Donnell with a smile and a wink. Donnell began to unclasp the white cloak with a mumbled apology, but Eochaid stayed his hand. "Hold on to it for now," he said, turning and pointing up the road. "There is much work to do here, and we must be quick. Come."

They began to hurry further up the road as a group. Up ahead was the small village square, and behind it, the looming Celtic Rock, that great black monolith with mysterious cup-and-ring carvings all around. The druids were standing in a circle staring inwards towards one another just below the great Rock, focused, as if they expected something to appear among them. Facing them, Donnell could make out Gabrán and the red-haired Fenella. Both looked calm – their faces expressionless.

However, nearby where they stood, on the small rise just above the square, something was very wrong. A group of Norsemen were gathered with spears at the ready, and appeared to have several local people tied up and held prisoner. These people were being advanced forward one at a time, at spearpoint. A smaller group of warriors, two axe men in black cloaks and a single spearman, were just a few feet from the circle of druids, pointing at them, weapons at the ready.

Just then there was a high scream from the street between them and the square, and Donnell saw that a girl aged around twelve had been struck to the ground outside a house, a Norseman standing over her with his spear pointed towards the child's neck. Donnell recognised the house as that of the crofter Niamh, one of several homes on the main street which sat in front of a small patch of land. Niamh herself was scrabbling to get at the Norseman, but was being held back by two other villagers, while her younger children stood clutching the hem of her skirts, and crying. On the opposite side of the street, at the blacksmith's place, a further Norseman stood guarding three grey horses which Donnell recognised as belonging to Ogledd, the village

Luftenand.

Without stopping to think, Donnell found himself swinging up into Beira's saddle, and spurring the horse forward, raising his hunting spear as he rode. He heard the running footsteps of his companions behind him.

Perhaps complacent of any sense of danger, the Norseman glanced up as he heard the hooves on the road, but it was far too late. He began to lift his spear up from where the girl was lying in front of him at just the moment that Donnell and Beira went crashing into him. The spear was knocked from the Norseman's hand and went shooting harmlessly across the road, while the man himself flew several feet through the air before crashing down to the ground, landing just in front of Beira, only to then be trampled beneath her hooves.

Donnell pulled up the horse and dismounted, his own spear still in hand, while the young girl got up and ran back to her mother. The belligerent Norse warrior was unconscious a few yards away.

Sahar and his other companions caught up, each one readying their weapons. The Norseman guard across the street initially pulled out an axe, but on seeing the number of foes that he faced, he turned and ran into the blacksmith's shop behind him.

* * *

"Noble, but hasty, my young friend," said Eochaid, briefly crouching to check the pulse of the fallen warrior. "Still, some bloodshed on the part of these invaders might be inevitable. Now, we must go to the druids. It is *essential* that we keep them safe. This way."

Eochaid hurried up towards the circle of druids; he remained incredibly spry for someone who to all appearances was a very old man. Bib, Malcolm and Sahar all followed, the latter readying her compact crossbow.

Donnell briefly looked round at Niamh, who had come over to thank him. He nodded, and give the young girl a pat on the cheek, too. On impulse, he passed Beira's reins to the child, asking the girl if she'd keep an eye on the horse for a short while. She nodded, eyes wide, and then smiled.

"Have you seen anything of Ogledd, or the Laird's mounted warriors who set out from Wherrycross?" Donnell asked Niamh.

The crofter glanced over towards the blacksmith's shop. "No sign of the Laird's men," she said. "But Ogledd is around here somewhere. I will get the children out of harm's way – and we can take Beira to our infield, if you like."

"Thank you both," said Donnell, and he hurried off to catch up with Malcolm and the others.

As he did so, Eochaid looked up, thoughtful, but kept walking in silence. Their arrival had clearly caught the attention of the gathering of Norse warriors who were standing on the knoll nearby, just beyond the village square. The Norsemen had stopped what they were doing, and assembled into a defensive formation, spears and axes at the ready, and the smaller group who had been approaching the druids now also moved closer to their companions. For some reason, though, the druids had barely stirred. They were still in a circle, staring towards one another. Donnell recognised all five druids from the forest, now; the leader Congal was closest to him with his back turned.

As their groups reached the druids, Donnell was surprised to hear the faintest of chanting, even although none of their mouths seemed to be moving. "Protect them," said Eochaid simply, looking to Malcolm. "None can harm them while the enchantment is underway, but the moment they stop they will be in danger. If anything happens to them now, all protection is lost."

"Very good," said Malcolm, somewhat blankly.

Eochaid looked to Sahar, who had stopped and loaded her crossbow.

She looked him in the eyes and nodded. "Understood. If any of the filth who serve Iohric the Ganger come any closer to this place, they fall with a bolt in one eye, or in both." Bib went to stand beside her too, unsheathing a dagger, but keeping his distance from Malcolm.

"What now?" Donnell asked. "How do we defeat them?"

"Perhaps the question should be 'do we defeat them - or even fight them at all?'" said Eochaid.

"What do you mean?"

"The tall Norseman is taking control of this place. That has been clear for some time. At first, I thought that their men were gearing up for war – an attack on Wherrycross, a slaughter of the locals, perhaps. But now it seems that they are trying to convert the population, perhaps as a way to begin to gain control of the entire area." Eochaid pointed at the cluster of Norse spearmen, and Donnell realised that the bound prisoners were being taken one at a time to a near-spherical silver artefact on the ground, which looked rather like an enormous rune-engraved coin. The Norse were watchful, but were neither coming closer to Donnell and his companions nor backing away. "They will ask them to swear fealty. All who refuse will be killed. But if the locals agree, then the Norse horde is larger and we are even more outnumbered. Is it wise to fight?"

"But they are capturing and threatening to kill people. My people."

"My village is full of the Norse scum, too," said Malcolm. "They are destroying the place, and forcing the locals to work as slaves for Iohric. They are gathering rocks, and starting to build fortifications."

"Well. And if they agree, they will simply be serving a different master from the current Laird."

"I can't believe I am hearing this, Eochaid," said Malcom. "You can't mean it. These people are monsters."

"Are they really?" asked the older man. "Do they look any different from you or I?"

"But Malcolm is right," Sahar interjected, walking towards the older man and frowning up at him. "I know these warriors – they are traitors to their people, exiles. They have no honour. Their loyalties are bought and sold by the wealthiest warlords, and they will reive lands and massacre the people simply for coin. When they are not starting wars or raiding villagers, they make their fortunes through slavery. I've tracked them down to here, and seen first-hand the damage they have done."

"I thought you said you were their prisoner," said Donnell quietly, frowning.

Sahar hesitated, looking up at him. "I am sorry, Donnell, to have misled you slightly. I was close to being taken prisoner, it's true. And they would certainly enslave and torture me, given the chance. But I came here by choice – to track down and kill Iohric. I need to get my revenge at any cost, for family and honour."

"So, you followed them?"

"I stowed away on the ship that you saw on the beach, and then destroyed it once we arrived. You must understand me – I have been tracking down the Ganger ever since he murdered my father, Hrólfr the Red. After that foul deed, Iohric fled, instead of paying the blood price for his crimes. I followed his path here. So, I say we must defeat them – the leader, at the very least, though all of his men deserve painful deaths for serving that monster."

"Such an interesting girl," said Eochaid, nodding, "and a valid story I am sure. But what would you say if the villagers were to fight off the Norsemen, and then get massacred by a wyvern? Would that be a price worth paying?"

There was silence for a moment.

Back down at the square, a group of men emerged from the black-smith's house. Donnell spotted the pompous Laird's Luftenand Ogledd, walking ahead of several Norse-looking armoured warriors, each of whom wore black cloaks and carried glittering axes that appeared freshly forged. Across the street, the crofter Niamh had already moved away behind her house, together with the horse and her three children.

"Cow dung. Ogledd's been captured," muttered Malcolm.

But Donnell watched in silence. Ogledd wasn't bound, and he didn't have the manner of a beaten man. He was walking with a spring in his step, and wearing another set of brightly coloured clothing, and a foolish-looking purple hat. Next, a familiar, hugely tall and armoured figure with long braided white hair emerged from the blacksmiths. Iohric. The huge warrior walked over to join Ogledd – and the Luftenand clapped him on the shoulder and smiled.

Confrontation

"Ogledd's nothing but a foul traitor," said Donnell, pointing. "Look. They've been working together." He took a step back, closing in beside his companions and in front of the druids as the new group of foes approached from the road.

Beside him, Donnell felt Sahar raising her crossbow, and he was sure she would fire at Iohric if she got a clear shot at him. "Wait for the right moment," he whispered. "If you shoot now, they'll all attack us. We need to get out of this alive."

"Donnell," shouted Ogledd, his nasal voice as confident as ever, walking just ahead of the Norsemen. "I seem to remember giving you instructions to travel northwards with… a message. I admit, it suited me to have you away from here." He snorted a strange squeak of a laugh. "But yet here you are. You are a traitor to your Luftenand and to all of this village."

"You are a fine one to talk of traitors, Ogledd," replied Donnell loudly, "It seems you have been helping these criminals. You are a coward and a fool. When the Laird's warriors come here from Wherrycross, you'll be hanged for working for them."

Ogledd advanced until he and the Norsemen were just a few paces away, and then stopped. Iohric looked even taller up close – the enormous Norseman stood a head above most of the other men, but appeared content to let the Luftenand do the talking for now.

"Working for them?" said Ogledd with a snort, and then he smirked. "Absolutely wrong. They are working for *me*. They are my guests, and will help to bring strength to this land. It's about time we had a new Laird, I think." Donnell recognised the faces of the two black-cloaked warriors closest to Ogledd. They were the 'cousins' he had recently been entertaining – now, apparently, revealed as two of Iohric's henchmen.

The Norse spearmen on the knoll above them had also moved closer, merging with Ogledd's men, and together they closed in on the small group of companions from below and above. At least the druids were behind them, Donnell thought to himself.

"We need to get out of here," said Malcolm, turning, a high note of panic entering his voice.

"No. Protect the druids," repeated Eochaid, sounding composed.

"Surely the druids will help us?"

Donnell turned to look behind them again, and suddenly realised that the whispered chanting had stopped. The druids were no longer making a sound. And they were no longer standing in a circle, either.

Gabrán, the intense black-haired druid to whom Donnell had spoken just the day before, was standing behind the tall leader of their group, Congal. And he held a long, curved dagger in his hand. As Donnell started to call out, Gabrán thrust the dagger deep into his leader's lower back, and then cruelly twisted it. There was a terrible grimace across his face, as if he both enjoyed and feared what he was doing.

Congal's mouth fell open in a gasp, his eyes popping in shock, and then he gave out a low, curdling cry that faded to nothing. He slumped to his knees and then fell forward, slipping cleanly off the dagger's blade, and hitting the ground with a sickening deathly thud.

* * *

"What are you doing?" yelled Eochaid, raising his sword, but the druid

Gabrán ignored him. He crouched and turned his victim's corpse, lifting the man's hand and ripping the ring with the white stone from the limp finger of his former comrade. The other three druids were huddled together looking aghast, Fenella in the middle with her arms around both of them, while Gabrán got up and walked towards the Norsemen, blood dripping from his hand and running down his wrist.

"I did as you asked," he said to Iohric. "Now I must have what I was promised. Release him to me."

Iohric muscled past the other warriors to the front of the group, sword in one hand and shield in the other. He began to reply to Gabrán, but at that moment there came an explosive noise like a boat crashing into a harbour wall, as Sahar had raised her crossbow and squeezed the trigger.

Seeing her move just in time, Iohric had raised his shield to block the shot. The impact gave off a flash like a miniature fork of lightning, and the bolt ricocheted off, embedding itself into Ogledd's upper arm. The Luftenand screamed and collapsed to the ground.

"Mmm," Iohric grunted, his voice like rocks rubbing together. "A coward's move, Sahar," he said, in a thick accent. "You disgrace your father by relying on this Moorish weapon."

Sahar had reloaded, but as she raised the weapon again, two of Iohric's cloaked comrades stepped forward, each holding axes up towards her neck. She froze, and then – as one of them barked a command in the Norse tongue – she slowly placed the weapon down by her feet. Other Norse warriors stepped up to Donnell and the others holding up spears, and, hopelessly outnumbered, they too put down their weapons.

Clipping his shield to his broad silver-studded belt, Iohric held out his left hand. "Now," he called out. "Let me see the prize."

Gabrán stepped towards the towering Norseman, whose pale blue eyes were like slits in the dim light, and then tentatively placed the bloodied ring in the man's huge palm.

There was a pause as everyone present looked at the large, ornate ring with its gem stone and mysterious triskelion carvings, and while most were no doubt unsure of its significance, one thing was very clear to all – the ring was the motive for murder.

* * *

Iohric nodded and closed his fingers round the ring, then reached down and placed it inside the coin pouch at his belt. After rummaging for a moment, he pulled a key out from the same pouch. "You want your payment, Celtish man? This is the key to the stronghold where your brother is locked," he said, lifting a long bronze key in the air. Gabrán reached for it, and without a second's hesitation, Iohric ran him through the throat with his sword. The druid slumped soundlessly to the ground. Donnell heard further gasps and wails from behind him, where the remaining druids were standing, and a small crowd of locals were also watching on, aghast, from the edge of the village square.

"Now," said Iohric, still holding the bloodied sword aloft, and looking round at Donnell and his companions. "Hand over that devil girl, and swear loyalty to me. Bring Loki's belt!"

Donnell watched as the large silver disc was rolled down from the rise to where they were standing. As it got closer, he saw that it was around the thickness of his thumb, and was slightly cup-shaped rather than being truly a disc. It was as wide as a milking bucket, and apparently quite heavy.

When the men had brought the object right up to where they stood, they carefully lowered it until it lay flat on the ground. The upper surface showed an image of one of the Norse gods in a triangle-shaped cloak and holding an axe, and this image was circled by two rings of runes.

As he watched on, Donnell realised that the féth fíada was now slowly fading. He then realised that due to the conflict with the Norse, he had momentarily forgotten about the wyvern. He glanced up to the sky, but still nothing could be seen above them, not even a common seagull.

He also realised that the boggle, Bib, was nowhere to be seen.

And could he hear hooves?

Iohric stepped forward again. He sheathed his sword, and began rubbing his shield arm, wincing. "Ah, your bolt hurt me, girl! As I said, that weapon is unworthy of a true warrior. But I will make you suffer for this soon enough." He looked around at the assembled people, and raised his voice to be heard by those who were clustered near the houses. "Now Celtish savages, it is time for you to swear. Become my servants, or you all die."

"I thought he was in charge," muttered Donnell, pointing at the prostrate, unconscious form of Ogledd in his now-bloodied robes. Iohric laughed, throwing his head back, and then kicked out at the Luftenand on the ground. "He was a poor host, but a useful liar," replied the Norseman, and his men also laughed, looking down at the fallen village chief.

The moment's distraction was enough for Sahar. She ducked under the axe blades in front of her, punching both foes in the face as she rose, and then twisting past them in a single move. Donnell saw her duck under the clutches of another Norseman who tried to grab at her, and as she stood back up, she had a knife in her right hand.

Attack

Advancing towards Iohric, Sahar dodged past another spearman and launched herself at the Norse leader, slashing out with the knife in her hand. The blade whipped past his face and left a deep gash on his cheek and forehead which began to spout blood; the move would have removed both his eyes if he hadn't leaned back just in time.

On her reverse stroke, she leaped up and hooked one arm around the huge warrior's neck, and then hammered the knife home into his shoulder. He bellowed and staggered backwards, blood flowing liberally from both his arm and face.

Iohric drew his sword again and stabbed upwards at her with the blade, but couldn't gain any distance or leverage to fully swing it at her. His men raised their weapons, but were unable to get a clear shot while the two foes were intertwined.

Sahar, meanwhile, ducked and dodged one jab after another from Iohric, until at last the flat of the blade did make firm contact with the back of her head, and she fell away from the man, reeling.

Malcolm had taken the opportunity to snatch up his great maul, and he smashed it down against the nearest Norseman, caving in the man's chest and sending him crashing backwards into one of his compatriots. Both of them collapsed to the ground. Taking his friend's lead, Donnell crouched down to lift his spear, and nearly lost his head as he rose – a sword swooshed through the air just above him. He rose and parried the next stroke and then tripped his attacker, kicking the man hard in the back of the head as he fell.

Hurrying backwards towards the surviving druids, Donnell took stock of the situation. Eochaid had also moved back up beside the druids. The old man had his sword raised, and Bib was now crouched by Congal's body, still wielding his own dagger. At present, though, the pair were not under attack.

Donnell looked up, noticing the sound of hooves again. The féth fíada had thinned almost to nothing now, and looking towards the northwest – the same way he had walked the previous morning towards Wallace's farm – he saw six armoured riders closing in fast. The Laird's warriors had arrived.

Malcolm was now being pinned back by three Norse attackers, and Donnell stepped forward to help him, knocking one of them backwards with his spear butt, and stabbing another in the leg, grounding the man. Looking up, he saw that Iohric had retreated from Sahar clutching at his wounds, and the young woman was now ferociously sparring with one of the 'cousins', a black-cloaked Norse warrior, with each coming close to stabbing the other in the face as Donnell watched on.

It appeared that Donnell wasn't the only one to see the arriving riders, however. Iohric and another two of his warriors turned and hurried off towards the blacksmith's shop, where the smoky grey horses were tethered. When they got there they mounted up, unopposed by any of the local onlookers, and set off down the main path towards Weir, gaining pace quickly. Soon they were galloping away, dwindling into the distance, leaving the majority of their men behind them.

Donnell turned and threw his spear full strength at the back of the warrior that was trading blows with Sahar. The spear missed his body, but the shaft caught him in the back of the neck, stunning him, and he fell to his knees with his hands up in a defensive position. Sahar deftly kicked the man's sword from his hand, and stood back.

And then the mounted warriors arrived.

* * *

The confrontation between the warriors of Wherrycross and the remaining Norsemen was fierce but brief. Once it was clear to all that Iohric had fled and that the only remaining black-cloaked lieutenant lay bleeding on the ground, the determination of the other fighters quickly evaporated. A few small pockets of spearmen resisted, but they were quickly overwhelmed by the superior speed and reach of the mounted warriors from Wherrycross.

Most of the surviving Norse surrendered quickly, and a number of them rapidly turned out to be press-ganged locals who had only recently sworn fealty upon Loki's belt; all of these fighters found their loyalties quickly relapsing.

Over by the carved rocks, Malcolm was lying on his back, groaning. He had taken a lengthy gash to his thigh during the fighting, and was trying to staunch the blood with a handful of grass. Donnell hurried over but Sahar moved in front of him, pulling out a small roll of canvas from inside her sealskin jerkin. She held it out to Donnell. "Want to patch up his wounds?"

"I don't have that skill," he said.

She sniffed. "Hmm. Fine. In truth, I'm no healer, either." The young Moor was splattered with blood herself, but most of it seemed to be Iohric's.

Then Donnell noticed another figure at his side – it was the druidess, Fenella.

"I'll see to this," she said, waving them both away, "and perhaps you can help finish this fight and restore peace to the village."

Donnell stood back and watched for a moment as the druidess

worked; he had not seen many healers, but her work seemed exceptionally neat and fast. She had several pouches at her waist, and an impressive range of small tools appeared in her hands, one after the other. Soon the wound was stitched, covered with a small bundle of herbs to staunch the blood, and strapped up. Malcolm thanked her and stood up, wincing.

Donnell turned and hurried over towards the square. He passed Eochaid and Bib, who were now covering up the body of the traitor druid Gabrán, and approached the mounted warriors who were galloping this way and that, rounding up and disarming the last of the opposition warriors into the village square, most of whom were now wounded and dispirited. It was best to get this over with, he thought, and find out if he was a fugitive to the Laird's men or not.

But as he approached their leader, he heard a shrill screeching noise from above, and his heart skipped. He looked up to see the now familiar slow circling of the wyvern.

* * *

Before long, most of those nearby had noticed it too. The riders from Wherrycross had stopped fighting and were trying to calm their horses; their dark-helmeted leader shouted crisp orders to his men to pull together into formation. Donnell hefted his spear in his hand and held it firmly in front of him, wondering if it would even make a scratch on the terrible creature's scaly hide.

He felt a presence by his side, and looked around to see Eochaid. The old sorcerer was looking up calmly, unarmed. He stared at the great winged beast as if looking at a curious new species of bird or insect, fingering a small object in his hand all the while. "A foolish act of bravery seems to be in order," he muttered. "Not really what I had in mind at the start."

Donnell looked back upwards, to see that the beast was just above them now. He could clearly make out its evil face – ridged eyes that gave way to horns, and massive bared teeth. Donnell crouched down, still gripping the spear. His heart was pounding faster than ever, and the familiar chill had returned. He focused on his own body position in order to try to distract himself from the mortal threat. He shifted the position of his feet slightly, keen to ensure that he remained balanced.

Could the creature's own momentum be its undoing, he briefly wondered? He had used the same technique to face down a boar charge many years ago – the injuries he sustained in doing so hadn't permanently crippled him – but still… this time, he knew on some level that to stand his ground was suicide.

Donnell looked down, and set his spear against the inside of one foot, holding the shaft as tightly as he could in both hands. After all, there seemed little point in throwing the weapon at the creature while it was airborne, but if it were to dive at him…

And then, that is exactly what the wyvern did, forming that distinctive, bunched, arrowhead-shaped position.

"Well, goodbye," muttered Eochaid, stepping beside him and raising one hand, at which point Donnell realised that old spellcaster was holding the brooch with the amber stone that he had seen Gabrán use in the forest. The old man twisted the stone inside the brooch between thumb and index finger, and a blinding flash of light rose up towards the creature. Donnell got the sense that the old man was collapsing, and simultaneously caught sight of something small flying past his face, and falling to the ground.

As he peered up through eyes that he had half closed against the light, Donnell saw that the wyvern had now changed course, coming out of its dive close above him and beginning to circle again, but much less elegantly. It was struggling like a bird caught in pondweed. It flailed out with first one wing and then the other, clearly out of balance as it floundered, trying to resume its circling hunting movement.

It looked to Donnell as if the creature was fighting something, battling an invisible current. And then he realised that he could make out something different upon its body – a glowing yellow line around the beast's neck, digging in like a noose.

He watched on for another minute or so as it tried to regain its balance, staying in the air but moving little. And then, with two enormous beats of its wings, it turned and departed northwards, flying only a few dozen feet above the ground but gradually rising.

It was a few moments before Donnell was fully paying attention to his surroundings again. He remembered that something had fallen to the ground ahead of him. Poking around in the grass with his toe, he again saw the round, carved brooch with the yellow stone. He realised that Eochaid must have stripped it from the traitor Gabrán, who now lay dead nearby.

What power did the object have? And what, indeed, was the power of its partner artefact, the ring with the white stone that was now in Iohric's possession? Too busy to consider these matters further, he crouched and picked the brooch up, putting it in his coin pouch for safe keeping.

Turning, he saw the shocked faces of a dozen nearby villagers, as people who had crouched down or hidden behind trees, rocks and walls were gradually emerging. Others were still sheltering in their homes, peeking out from nearly every door. But much closer, a familiar figure lay upon the ground.

Eochaid.

Shouting for the druidess Fenella, Donnell hurried over to the spellcaster. The man looked peaceful, his face unmoving.

As Donnell approached, there was a streak of blue from his left, and Bib arrived at the man's prostrate body first, crouching by Eochaid's head and feeling for a pulse. Donnell stopped, looking down at the little boggle with a sinking feeling. Soon, Fenella and a few others had joined him.

Bib looked up, directing his attention at Fenella. "He's alive, druidess – at least I think so."

"Take him to the village Greathouse," she said. "Let all the injured be taken there." She spun, her long curly red hair whipping around as she did so. "Soldiers!"

Two of the Laird's men rode over and dismounted. At her direction, they stooped, and carefully lifted Eochaid. Fenella walked alongside, trying to get a response from the old man, and most of the others followed a short distance after.

A Proposition

The Laird's riders resumed their work of rounding up the remaining Norse belligerents, bringing the band of surrendering prisoners together in the village square. The grievously wounded were taken to the Greathouse with Eochaid and kept under guard.

A number of the locals were now watching curiously from the area outside the blacksmith's, daring to come closer than before. Leaving the soldiers to the work of tying up the captives, Donnell crossed back towards Niamh's croft. He thanked the woman, and asked after both the children and Beira.

The woman nodded, barely looking at him as she scanned the sky with a frown. "Aye. Your horse is well secured at the back, and can stay there as long as you need. And I kept the children inside. My girls are brave, but this… it's not normal. Things are changing for the worse in this land, I feel."

"Perhaps, my friend. But I think the main danger has passed for now," he replied, following her gaze and then pointing over to the village square. "The Laird's men are seeing to the Norse raiders, and the old spellcaster Eochaid did something to ward off that great beast, the wyvern. He was badly hurt in doing so, though, and the druidess of Brighid is attending him now. I think he has been mortally wounded, for I saw…"

She glanced at him as he tailed off, but didn't press the matter. Just then the children emerged and clung to their mother's side as she spoke to Donnell, tugging at her coat and asking rapid questions. The youngsters seemed to have fully recovered from any fright they had received, and even the girl who had been threatened by the Norse warrior smiled as she saw the Laird's soldiers riding around on their fine horses.

As the young family made moves to go and check upon their neighbours, Donnell thanked them again for their help, and moved on, suddenly feeling anew the multiple pains in his body from the mistreatment the day before. He stretched and rubbed his arms and back, then crossed the street and ducked inside the blacksmith's shop. It was a building he knew well; the blacksmith, Willem, was Malcolm's father. However, Malcolm himself had a very difficult relationship with his father, and since the young man's courting of Alna, the two kinsmen had barely spoken.

Inside, the place was as dirty as ever, soot covering every surface. The huge forge was glowing gently at the centre of the room. A clutter of objects and weapons, damaged and new alike, sat on a wooden table to one side, with the anvil standing in between the table and forge. There was another table at the near side of the room with two pails of water on it. Closer to the back of the room were numerous chairs and barrels, and the walls were adorned with horseshoes and farming tools. A ladder led up to the loft.

Willem stood by the anvil and looked up as Donnell walked in.

"Thought you might be the Norsemen come back," he said gruffly.

"They have gone, defeated by the Laird's men. You should take a look outside. And you should know as well, Willem, that Alna has gone with the Norsemen. She is gone for good, I think, having sworn loyalty to those people, as have many of her folk from Weir. Malcolm is taking it very hard, and it will be difficult for some time to come, I expect."

"Mmm. As you would expect, I suppose, those fools from Weir taking up with such people." The old man stepped over to the forge, and prodded at it with a long iron shovel for a good long while, the reflection of its glow dancing in his eyes as he thought this over. "They were cold men, those Norse, but they didn't mistreat me," he said at last. "That tall warrior, I think he will be a fearsome ruler some day."

"I think that is his belief, too," Donnell said with a frown. "He has suffered a defeat and been wounded too, but it's likely that we haven't seen the last of him. He still controls Weir, and may assault our village again once his forces have rebuilt their strength. We in Cardhu need to act to protect ourselves."

"Then I suppose I shall be called on to arm the villagers. Which is no different from what the Norse were asking of me. Forge swords, repair ancient weapons."

"What's that about ancient weapons?" asked Donnell. "What did they ask you to do?"

"It was an axe, a huge one. The weapon of a legendary Norse king. It needed to be repaired, and they have plans for it I think. I have to admit, it was a fine piece of work."

"Is it something that could be used against us?"

The man turned, and leaned on the great anvil. "They asked about joining it with an item of power. A ring of some kind. I'm no jeweller, so I can tell you nothing more than I told them. If this ring truly is enchanted, then it will be difficult to work with without destroying it. Perhaps impossible."

Just then, a familiar outline darkened the door. Malcolm hesitated, then walked in, with Sahar just behind him. Donnell's old friend looked pale, but with his wound now neatly dressed, he was barely limping.

Breaking off from the conversation and making a mental note to return to the matter, Donnell crossed over to his friend and put one arm on the man's shoulder. "Shouldn't you be getting some rest?" he asked.

Malcolm looked around the room without responding to this suggestion. "May I?" he asked, pointing to a chair close to the door, and looked up at Willem. The father gave a grudging nod, and the son sat, putting his weapon down at his feet.

"Who is this new foreign wench?" asked Willem, pointing rudely at Sahar. "Another heretic you've taken up with?"

Malcolm scowled, and Sahar flipped her knife in her hand and gave him a cold look, but Donnell walked over to Willem and held his hands up, palms together. "Don't push your boy away, sir," he said. "We three have just walked away alive from a battlefield, and Malcolm's woman has left to be with the enemy. It's a time for us to talk of peace and coming together."

The old blacksmith grunted, and said nothing for a moment. Then he stood, eyes narrowed as if suppressing anger, and Donnell wondered if he was about to walk away. Instead, though, he walked over to his son, and proffered his hand. "The lad is right," he said. "And it gives me no pleasure to say that I was, too, when I warned you about the folk of Weir. Will you return to us and to Cardhu, son?"

Malcolm was shaking as he extended his arm, looking more upset than ever.

"I'm Sahar, by the way. I just saved both of their lives," said the young woman with a slight smile at Willem. "Pleased to meet you, and you're welcome."

The old man nodded slowly. "Well met. Times are changing – whether for the better or worse, we are yet to see. But let not the old traditions die too quickly. It's time to speak to the neighbours, and share bread and ale."

Donnell left the others to these preparations and stepped outside, where he was joined again by Niamh's family across the street, as well as several other locals who had emerged from hiding. The prisoners had by now all been disarmed and locked in the closest barn. Indeed, it was lively in the village square, now, and the relief that the locals felt could easily be seen written across their faces.

** * **

The Wherrycross warriors had dismounted, and villagers were showing their appreciation by offering them food and seeing to their horses, with some also presenting small gifts. With the men's helmets off, Donnell realised that he recognised the leading warrior – it was the dark-haired man who had ridden by the King's side into Wherrycross. He was holding the reins of a powerful-looking black stallion.

"My lord," said Donnell with a brief bow. "My name is Donnell, and I'm a native of Cardhu. Thank you for your help. You saved the village."

"Ah, Donnell – the fugitive messenger. I came to apprehend you," said the warrior, reaching for his sword hilt, and Donnell took a step back, ready to flee.

But then the man gave a hearty laugh, letting his sword swing free in its sheath, and clapping his hands together. "Relax, man. I owe you my thanks, in fact. I am the one they call Mac Rath. Or to be accurate, most people around here probably call me the Laird's bastard. I was born to a servant at Dumbarton Castle, but it's well known to all that my true father is the Laird of Wherrycross and Cunninghame."

Donnell suddenly remembered Bib's description of the man, which seemed to be at least partly false. The warrior wasn't wearing Northumbrian armour but rather a light ring mail, and had a friendly smile for someone with his dark reputation. He could be no older than twenty summers, and must have been a child in the Laird's household when Donnell himself had trained there. Now, however, there could be no doubt that the young man was a capable warrior, and a confident leader.

"Walk with me a while," said Mac Rath, indicating the direction with a nod. Donnell followed as the armoured man led his black horse over to a patch of grass by the side of the village square.

"I realised that you had not travelled northwards to deliver my father's message, it's true. But I am not sure that the Laird of Inverkip would have had time to ride south in any case, even had he been willing to do so. The royal party hunted and drank ale, and they will return to the royal seat at Dumbarton with the issue of succession undecided in my uncle's absence.

"But this just means that the clan won't agree on a successor to my father's seat during the King's visit. It will happen in due course, and although my father is sickly and childless, he is not in any immediate danger."

"You spent time with the King, then?" Donnell was awed at the very prospect.

The warrior patted his horse, then ran his hand down its nose. "Of course. I am very familiar with the court. King Arthgal's son is my childhood friend, and we played together as boys and hunted the glens of Lennox in recent years."

"I see," said Donnell, rather unsure of the significance of this information.

"The King knows and trusts me," continued Mac Rath "I grew up in his household, and I believe he would be happy to see me inherit these lands. But still, I am certain that he did not plan to deny the legitimacy of the Laird's brother as the heir to Laird Owain and their clan. That would be too much of a risk – it would be seen as a threat to the other Lairds. If he could replace one of them with his man, he could replace any, you see."

The young warrior looked around at the village, falling silent for a moment. Donnell looked over towards the Celtic Rock, and saw that a blanket had been pulled across the body of the former druid leader,

Congal. Two of the other surviving druids were sitting close by to it with heads bowed, with only the red-headed Fenella absent.

"And so," Mac Rath continued, "some might say that the longer this remains unresolved, the better it is for me. So, I don't feel any bitterness towards you at all, Donnell. My uncle might feel very differently, for he undoubtedly wants to rule over both realms."

Donnell nodded; it certainly didn't feel like he deserved any thanks for this outcome, such as it was.

"In truth, you were not the reason that I set out. When we realised there were Norsemen at large, I took a squad of my best men. We destroyed the smaller ship boat that arrived on the beach, saw the heathens off, then rode hard for Cardhu. We were close by when that devilish mist descended, blocking us from making our way into the village."

"It was the work of the druids, my lord. They were protecting us from the wyvern. Or, at least, I thought they were…"

He suddenly remembered Caelia's words about treachery, and wondered about when Gabrán's plotting with Iohric had begun. It then occurred to him that the druids couldn't have travelled to Cardhu in the time after he had seen the wyvern above the sea – and in any case, they wouldn't have seen the beast from their forest home.

"On reflection," he added, "they may have been here to stop you. The druids can be trusted, but there was a traitor among their circle. Now he lies dead."

"And here we are in victory," said Mac Rath, stretching out his arms. "The beast has fled in terror before us, too. Now I had best lead my men back to the town and to my castle beyond before night falls."

"Can we accompany you part of the way?"

Mac Rath smiled. "It's very noble of you, woodsman. But these are my finest warriors, and I don't think the Norse will try their hand again today. I have two things to ask of you, though. First, of course, spread the news far and wide of our bravery and prowess today. It may not be the largest of battles, but it is encouraging to our people if they hear tales of a victory nonetheless, and it keeps our enemies wary."

"I will," said Donnell.

"And, well…" he paused, and caught Donnell's eye. "We are going to need a new Laird's Luftenand for this village. I think my father would approve if I made the appointment, at least on a temporary basis."

Donnell looked back at Mac Rath. The nobleman's eyes were a searching dark blue, and his forehead wrinkled into an earnest frown when he spoke. "You are clearly resourceful," Mac Rath continued, "and highly thought of in these parts, too. You could be a leader to these people. What do you say to the role?"

A momentary thrill came over Donnell at the offer, and as he pondered the prospect for a moment, he began to consider Malcolm's words about his own potential as a leader, and his friend's pronouncements that people would listen to him.

But on the other hand, is that really what he wanted? Didn't he spend most of his time trying to get away from the bustle and the demands of Cardhu decision making, and longing to be alone in the forest?

He didn't want to be a farm hand, that was certain, but the role of Luftenhand had many of the same issues – just on a larger scale. It was a role for an organiser, a central figure among the villagers. Someone who could be the heart and soul of their community, especially when it was under threat.

And that just waasn't him.

"I'm honoured, my lord, but I don't think I can represent and lead the people of Cardhu. I am just a woodsman by trade, and at present I am working to repay the debt that my parents owed to the farmer Tarin."

He looked back at Mac Rath, raising his hands to his chest. "I'll lend what support I can in repairing the defences, of course, and perhaps I can train some of the youngsters to defend themselves in the weeks to come. But I am not the right person to be the Luftenand."

"Very well." Mac Rath gave a single nod, and didn't appear annoyed at Donnell's reluctance, and nor did he try to persuade him to change his mind.

"However," Donnell continued, "if you are willing to take the opinion of someone born and raised here, I would recommend Niamh, the crofter woman who lives across from the blacksmith's forge. She's brave and wise, and a great organiser. Everyone in the village respects her."

"I see. Well then, I will speak with her before I leave. Fare well, Donnell, and speak again soon, gods willing. I'll return before long, and will ensure that the coastal road is better patrolled."

"That would be greatly appreciated. The Norse have been seen off, but I fear they will return."

"Indeed." Mac Rath began to walk away, and then hesitated, looking back at Donnell. "Oh, and about that message – I suppose you were to be paid for your work?"

Donnell's heart sank at the reminder that he had now missed out on the opportunity to free himself early from his servitude to Tarin. It surely would not come again.

"Yes," he replied. "Though of course, I don't expect to receive the payment from Macswain now. I made my choice; I decided to come here and be with my people, instead of continuing with the journey. I was already paid five groats as an advance, and I will of course return those as soon as I am able."

Mac Rath pursed his lips, and then shook his head sharply. "There is no need for that, Donnell," he said. "Keep the money. I will speak to the huntsmaster about it, and reimburse her myself if need be. I think that your actions today deserve some reward and recognition. But tell me – what were you due to receive on completion of your journey?"

"Well, some further coin, and also..." Donnell hesitated, struggling to find the words. He then glanced around in the direction of Tarin's farm, and then back at the young knight. Now that Cardhu was safer, he found it hard to face the fact that his chance of freedom was gone. "Macswain also suggested to me," he continued, staring at the groung as he spoke, "that the Laird might intercede with the farmer Tarin. I have spent many years working for him in order to pay off an old family debt."

"I see." Mac Rath paused for a moment, and then nodded. "Well, I can't promise that my father will listen to me. But I will certainly mention your name in connection with this debt. Even if you will not be the new Luftenand, I have a strong feeling that the village might have more need of your services, and not for farming. Dangerous times lie ahead of us."

Donnell stood silently at this, his mind buzzing with possible responses. "I don't expect to get something for nothing," he said at last. "I have worked hard to pay off my family's debt, and I am willing to do more yet."

"Understood."

"So, the Laird..." began Donnell, frowning. But before he could ask for any further clarification of what Mac Rath was proposing, the nobleman gave a cheerful wave and hurried off, leading his horse back down the main street to the village square, where his soldiers were starting to relax a little too much with some of the locals.

And it wasn't long before the group of warriors mounted up and set off back towards Wherrycross, taking with them Ogledd and the wounded black-cloaked Norse captain, but leaving behind the other prisoners to be used for any future bargaining with the Norsemen. As he watched them ride off, it occurred to Donnell that he should have given the note itself back to Mac Rath, to be returned to his father the Laird when he spoke to him. He touched briefly at the small slip of parchment in his pocket.

Well. It would have to wait. And perhaps, as the young nobleman had said, it didn't matter any more.

Donnell saw Bib walking towards the Celtic Rock, hood raised high, and crossed to intercept the little boggle. "I'm sorry about your master," he said. "Is there any hope?"

Bib pulled back his blue hood and smiled. "Yes. Master has awoken. He is strong and resourceful, and although he was badly weakened, I am confident that he will be himself again soon. The healer seems to share my optimism."

"That's wonderful news."

"Indeed, he wishes to take his leave as soon as he is strong enough to travel. I, of course, will not be remaining here – these people won't want to celebrate with my kind."

"I understand."

"After Eochaid has had some time to rest and heal, you should come and see us in Wherrycross, Donnell – you know the house."

The little creature began to leave, and Donnell suddenly remembered about the pony. As if reading his mind, Bib turned and said, "Yes, the violent grey pony will be there too, you'll see. Make sure you do come – before the season's end."

With that, he walked away.

* * *

Thank you for reading The Broken Circle - I hope you enjoyed it. Read on for an extract from **The Twisted Forest**, *the next book in The Druid Stones Saga*

AD 869, summer

A ragged line of riders was silhouetted against the sinking sun.

As the great island mountains turned to shadows against the late afternoon glow and sunlight reflected off the waves, Donnell held up one hand to shield his eyes from the glare. There was still no sign of movement from their Norse foes on the shoreside road below where he stood, though he was unable to see the occupied village of Weir from this far inland.

He turned and gestured, and the half dozen novice troops picked up their spears again and swung their horses around, each turning at a slightly different angle and forming into a careless-looking line. Donnell sighed, and spurred Beira closer, then passed in front of the small line of troops.

"Your spear has slipped from your stirrup," he said to the first, pointing. The boy Óengus was a promising horseman and strong of arm, although still too young to head a household of his own. The lad nodded, and adjusted the unfamiliar weapon.

The next pair were older, experienced in the saddle but no soldiers, nor would they ever be. They did the minimum required at each training session, then returned to their crofts and families as early as possible. Donnell nodded slightly and passed them by.

The next figure was a real soldier, broad and steady in the saddle. Erik was a former Norse warrior who had stayed in Cardhu after being injured at the battle months before. While most of his surviving fellows had been exchanged with the Norse for the food and metalware that the outsiders seemed to have in abundance, Erik had sworn allegiance to the village and to the Laird, and promised to fight for them if called upon. A muscular man with a short blonde beard and cropped hair, he had no family across on the islands, he said, and no love for the Norse leader Iohric or his henchmen. Donnell wasn't certain about the young man's loyalty over the long-term, but for now he was easy company, and a helpful example for the others to mimic.

"Good work, Erik," Donnell remarked, before turning and giving a few pointers to the older pair. The riders charged once more against their imaginary targets, and then Donnell had them dismount and dismissed the group for the evening.

Turning, he spurred Beira forward, but Erik came alongside him. "Touring the defences, chief?" said the man. "I'll come with you if want the company."

Donnell nodded. It hadn't escaped the men of the fledgling cavalry troop that he preferred his own company, but he appreciated their occasional efforts to bond with him.

"I would be happy for it. I'm going along the forest edge first, then down to check on the new wall. Do your best to keep up."

Donnell spurred the great chestnut mare towards the tops of the village, where there were larger outfields of sheep and cattle, on poorer, hilly terrain. Here, a long line of trees on the higher ground marked the extent of the crofters' lands.

With Erik riding just behind, he then followed a newly constructed path that ran between the drystane wall and the trees. After a couple of boggle attacks in which livestock and tools had been stolen, defences had been improved here too, even although it was in the opposite direction to the new Norse camp. On the orders of Niamh, the Laird's new Luftenand, the walls had been raised to chest height, and had been reinforced with a wooden tower every couple of hundred paces, three in all. People had come to refer to this new structure as the East Wall. It was clear to see where numerous trees had been felled to build these and other areas of the improved defences of the small community, leaving a broad cleared area between the East Wall and Holm's Wood itself.

As Donnell rode, he glanced down and patted Beira's flank with a smile. Whether or not the young nobleman Mac Rath had interceded on his behalf after the Battle of Cardhu, he did not know. But one way or another, the farmer Tarin had received word from the Laird's household that Donnell's debt had been cancelled, and that the former woodsman should be released to help Niamh to prepare Cardhu's defences.

Tarin had been furious, of course, and his anger had deepened when Donnell had then advised Niamh to requisition all of the farmer's horses to help with the defence of the village, and she had agreed. In a rage, Tarin had turned Donnell out of his previous lodging behind the stables – despite outrage from some of the other villagers at this treatment – and had also refused to allow the horses to be stabled there any more.

Now each horse was being looked after by its own rider, and Donnell was living in one of the outbuildings behind the blacksmith's shop, sharing this makeshift accommodation with Malcolm. It was little more than a shed, but he and Malcolm had taken the time to fix it up, repairing holes in the roof and walls. Malcolm in particular had a lot of skills with stone and woodwork, and together they had done an efficient job.

Donnell and Erik now continued to ride past the East Wall until the path turned down towards the ancient earthworks that marked older defences at the north of the village. These had now been reinforced with spiked branches along their length to make it near-impossible for troops or horses to approach from the shore.

"How are your fellows getting on?" Donnell asked, slowing Beira's pace to a walk as they approached the end of this part of their route.

Erik wasn't alone in having changed sides – another three Norseman had been badly wounded in the springtime battle, and had been nursed back to health by the druidess Fenella. They said they wanted to show their gratitude; they would leave back to the islands the following summer, but for now they were among the volunteer foot soldiers who were being trained and guided by Malcolm. As with the mounted troops, these troops were a mixed bunch, mostly farmers and youths, but were gradually learning the skills that they might need to defend the village. The sooner Cardhu could protect itself from attack, Donnell thought, the sooner he could relax.

"Those three are slow and stupid," said Erik, and he gave a short laugh. "That's why they got themselves injured."

"Maybe," said Donnell. "You think we shouldn't use them as mercenaries?"

Erik smiled again, and nodded. "Use them. Just make sure you send them in to battle first," he said. "Maybe their ugly faces will distract your enemies. Talking of which," Erik added, pointing downwards.

They had reached a vantage point on a rocky bluff above the burn, from where the settlements down at the shore could be easily seen. When Donnell and his companions had exchanged the remainder of the prisoners with the Norsemen who had settled there, Weir was little more than a fishing village. Iohric and his troops had retreated there and some of the local fishermen were now part of their horde, with Norsemen also reportedly marrying local women.

Now, there was a near-complete stone keep in a raised site at the top of the village, in the same place that a fortress had been abandoned by ancient people many generations before, and which had been little more than a set of stone ruins during Donnell's childhood. It was clearly a strategic position, and would allow Iohric and his men to watch for any vessels that travelled North or South, and perhaps prey on weaker targets, especially if they worked together with their kinsmen on the nearby islands.

One person in Cardhu was particularly suspicious about the uneasy truce with the Norse. The young woman Sahar – who Donnell had met and allied with when defending the village back in the springtime – had remained there, still hoping for an opportunity to exact her revenge on Iohric. Sahar had suggested that the only thing that had saved the locals from a bloodier conquest was that Iohric simply didn't have enough men after his losses from battle, in addition to losing two longships on the same day. However things had been relatively quiet after an initial exchange of prisoners, and there were now plans to trade with the Norsemen for much-needed supplies of fish and iron ore.

Donnell looked to where Erik was pointing. A dozen or so Norsemen, on foot, had emerged from the keep, and were gathered on the main Laird's road that ran up the coastline. Meanwhile, four mounted soldiers were closing in on them, riding north from Wherrycross, where the Laird of the area lived. Donnell was reminded of the band of soldiers led by Mac Rath who had ridden north and battled the Norse here in Cardhu a few months before.

Donnell dismounted, taking Beira by the reins and walking closer to the cliff edge; Erik did likewise. Donnell was generally considered to be tall, but the younger man stood a hand's breadth above than him as they looked down towards Weir.

The four mounted soldiers on the road had stopped, remaining on their horses. They cast long shadows in the evening light. The men were armoured and had shields, and for a moment Donnell wondered if battle would commence once more. However, instead, the two sides appeared to be talking. After a couple of minutes, the Laird's men turned their steeds and began to ride down the road, back towards Wherrycross.

* * *

"I wonder what that was…" Donnell began, but suddenly Erik's horse shied from something at its feet. It veered sideways towards where Donnell stood; he dodged out of the way, but overbalanced towards the cliff's edge. He felt a firm hand on his arm, and steadied, taking a step back from the edge. "I'm fine," he snapped, pulling his arm away, and then wondered why he hadn't just thanked the man.

Erik, however, was looking at the ground. He had pulled a knife from his belt. "Stand up, fiend!" he growled.

Donnell also looked down, grasping the pommel of the short sword which he now wore, and saw a familiar face crouching in the shadows. "Wait a moment, Erik," he said, putting one hand on the man's muscular arm. "This one is all right. I know him."

The mysterious little boggle who went by the name of Bib stood up in front of them and then bowed to the two men with a grin. "I see Cardhu is very much better defended these days. I can't shimmy up a hillside without having a knife pointed at me." His purple eyes gleamed with what could have been mirth or anger – it was difficult to say which.

"It's good to see you, Bib," said Donnell, not commenting on the creature's unconventional entry point, or how and why he had passed the other defences. The boggle, Donnell knew, couldn't always walk major paths without attracting unwelcome attention. "What news?"

"This little troll is with you?" Erik said, flipping his knife in one hand and then neatly slipping it back into its sheath. "You are a witch-man, in truth."

"No, he's not with me, nor a servant of mine," Donnell said. "I know very little of the ways of these boggles. The others of his kind you should be very wary of. They mostly haunt the forest; a group of them captured and tormented me for sport not long ago. But I know that Bib, here, is one that can be trusted."

Bib bowed at the compliment, his blue travelling hood falling across his face as he did so. Then he walked past them to the grassy area behind the bluff, where a low wall marked the edge of a sheep pasture. He hopped up onto the wall, and sat. "Much news from the south, he said. The Laird is mustering many troops".

"We just saw some. Will he move against the Norsemen? If so, we need to know his plans."

Bib inclined his head. "I believe that will happen eventually," he said. "And Eochaid?"

Bib smiled slightly. "My master is much recovered from his ordeal in

Cardhu."

"That's wonderful news," replied Donnell, walking forward towards the wall. "And in good health?"

The boggle hesitated. "Eochaid was very ill when he returned from here back in the springtime. After that, he slept for many days, pale and sickly looking, sweating and filled with dark visions. When he woke, he seemed to be back to his normal self, but I was too optimistic at first. Normally he… Well, let us just say that he has recovered. But it was a slow process. The events took their toll."

The little creature seemed much less sure of himself than Donnell remembered from their previous meetings. He nodded and said, "Please, pass on my wishes. I know I said I will visit, and I certainly still intend to."

Bib cocked his head and narrowed his eyes slightly. "I was actually sent to see the apothecary today, but when I saw you, I thought I would remind you about this visit." He shrugged. "Yes, come to Wherrycross. There is much to discuss. After another week or two, I am hopeful, he will be well enough to receive you."

"Agreed. And can I help with anything?"

The boggle sniffed and looked towards the village. "You can tell me where I might find the red-haired druidess."

When Bib had gone on his way, Donnell completed his circuit of the defences, still accompanied by Erik. Two new stone watchtowers were under construction by the main route between Weir village and Cardhu, though progress was slow, and the mason was arguing with a group of youths who had been helping. Erik and Donnell agreed to meet there the next day in the mid-morning to lend a hand; Erik was due to patrol first thing, while Donnell was required to meet with the village council. The two men then went their separate ways. Donnell had to make his way back towards the wooden watchtowers where he was due to take his turn on guard duty, but first he needed to leave

Beira safe and secure overnight.

As he rode, he started to feel the fatigue of the training session course through his body. At least there had been no further wyvern sightings, he thought to himself. Perhaps the great flying beast was truly dead by Eochaid's hand, or had somehow been compelled to return to its home in the north for a generation.

But more sightings of these creatures of dread seemed all too possible in the current times.

Want to read on? Find out more at www.jfdanskin.com.

THE DRUID STONES SAGA BOOK 2
THE TWISTED FOREST
J.F. DANSKIN

FREE - The Bonding

If you enjoyed *The Broken Circle*, why not sign up to my mailing list for news and behind the scenes extras, including a prequel novella set in the Druid Stones world.

The Bonding (A Druid Stones Story)

When you are chosen – what choice do you have?

Scotland: 9th century. Two friends await their traditional community bonding ceremony. Donnell thinks he knows his fate, while his friend Malcolm anticipates rejection. Haunted by a mystical encounter in the woods, both young men embark separately on their apprenticeships: Donnell with a mixture of excitement and guilt, and Malcolm with resignation – and a lasting bitterness. When fate brings them together again on a quest to find a renegade druid, Donnell's choices could affect the future of the realm – and directly threaten his own future too.

Scottish mythology and ancient Celtic lore meet historical fantasy in this prequel novella to the whole Druid Stones Saga.

Download your free copy here by visiting https://BookHip.com/JKLSDR

By submitting your email address, you consent to be added to my mailing list where you will receive writing news, free stories and information about new releases. You can unsubscribe at any time by following the link in the email.

Author note

This was the first Druid Stones story that I wrote – before *The Bonding*, and before I had planned the later novels in any detail. I wanted a story that was fast-paced, and which combined historical elements – an ancient Celtic kingdom at a time of Norse incursions – with fantasy elements that were based on Celtic myth. And I knew from a very early stage that it would be a series of five books, and that the magic of the druids would play a key role.

I began writing The Broken Circle in March 2019, in Scotland, and the story, too, portrays springtime. It was helpful for me to experience the sights and sounds of Scotland as I wrote, looking around at the trees, the shore, the weather. It may be a very different era, but the natural world is still quite similar!

Historical notes on The Broken Circle

Armour and weapons - I have kept the armour and weapons realistic and plausible for the period of time. In the 9th Century, ordinary folk would not have been riding around in plate armour or even chainmail! Norse raiders would have had access to metal armour, and it's likely that they used it.

Boggles - this word has the same origin as goblin or bogeyman. Some legends portray them as gremlin-like creatures, others as fairies, and still others as skeletons or undead. My representation here is rather like classic fantasy goblins, but I wanted to use the traditional Scottish word.

Cardhu, Weir and Wherrycross - these are fictional places, set on the west coast of Scotland in what would, in the 9th Century, have been part of the domain known as Ystrad Clud (see below). However, many of the other places more briefly mentioned are real and still exist today, such as Dumbarton Castle and the Isle of Arran. More on this in later books in the series!

Druids - druids were a major feature of Celtic culture and religion prior to the Christian era (see below). They were spiritual leaders, storytellers, and advisors to kings and warriors. However, by the time of our stories, their influence was diminishing.

The Norse - the period of time described in the book was close to the height of Norse power and influence on mainland Great Britain and Ireland. By this stage, they had captured York and Dublin, were in control of Normandy, and within a generation they would be laying siege to Paris. This is the era in which Alfred the Great of England made his reputation by taking a stand against the 'heathens'. Having initially focused on raiding, the Norse were by this time also establishing colonies on mainland Britain, and I wanted to reflect that in the book with the Norse attempting to take over of the village of Weir.

Religion - in this period of history, Christianity was well established, having spread from Ireland to the British mainland via a monastery on the Isle of Iona. However, traditional beliefs are likely to have survived for some time after this – there aren't enough historical records to be sure how much. I portray a kingdom where the kings and nobles follow Christianity as do some communities, but the bulk of the populace still revere the Celtic gods.

Wyverns - this classic mythic beast appears very often in early medieval images such as books and flags.

Ystrad Clud - this is a real, historical kingdom. In the 9th Century, Scotland had not yet emerged as a unified kingdom. Instead, the land was divided between 5 powers: Ystrad Clud (in the southwest), Dal Riada (a Gaelic-speaking realm in the northwest), Pictland (in the east), Northumbria (in the southeast, and extending into modern-day England), and the Norse realm (which controlled most of the islands but little of the mainland). The Druid Stones Saga is largely set in Ystrad Clud, but all of the other realms – or characters from them – feature in the books.

Also by J.F. Danskin

The Druid Stones Saga 2: The Twisted Forest

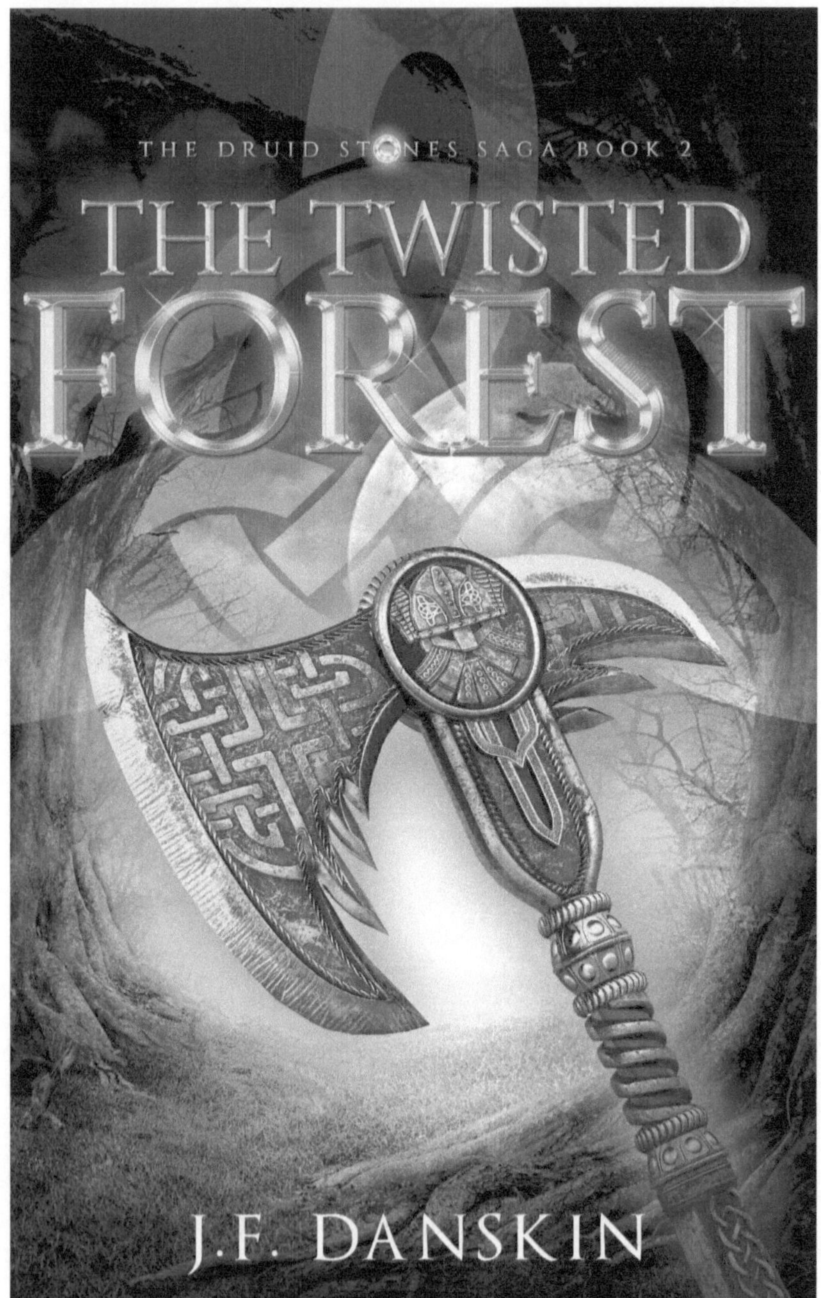
THE DRUID STONES SAGA BOOK 2
THE TWISTED FOREST
J.F. DANSKIN

Malevolent magic rises in the forest. Will Donnell's own growing powers be enough to meet the threat?

It has been a few months since the Battle of Cardhu. Donnell is preparing the villagers, anticipating further incursions from the Norse encampment on the coast. But the attacks, when they come, are from Donnell's beloved forest. What is causing normally peaceful beasts to behave in this way? Who is equipping the boggles with bows?

Healer Fenella wants to retrieve the stolen white stone of Lugh. Balance won't be restored until her circle of druids is reformed. Donnell is torn – Cardhu is vulnerable. The stone lies in the hands of the enemy Iohric: retrieving it will be a perilous mission. But when they find out what he intends to do with it, there doesn't seem to be much choice at all.

The thrilling second installment of the Druid Stones Saga.

Available at your preferred store here **https://books2read.com/Dru idStones2**

The Druid Stones Saga 3: The Mythic Spear

An ancient weapon. An advancing army. And five banished companions each facing their greatest struggle yet.

With their protector Mac Rath away at war, life at Castlecraik is frustrating for Donnell and his friends. Hunting boggles in the forest brings them no closer to their goal of finding the missing druid stone – and rebuilding the circle of druids.

When the young nobleman returns, it is clear that he has his own reasons for taking them into his household. The quest: to retrieve the legendary weapon from the ruins of Anwen's Cairn, deep within the forest. But no sooner have they set out than the great Norse dragonships of an invading army begin to arrive. Can the companions find what they are looking for – and do so in time to save their people?

Available at your preferred store here **https://books2read.com/Dr uidStones3**

The Druid Stones Saga 4: The Winter Tower

A renewed Norse threat and an army of Picts raise the stakes as winter descends on the kingdom.

Cardhu is lost to the Norse. Further inland a new settlement grows, in the shadow of a ruined tower with a history of its own. At last it seems as if the druid stones will be together again, allowing the place to be protected. But before the spell is cast, the druidess Méabh is abducted, forcing Donnell and his companions on a treacherous journey towards the great capital – where new armies gather.

Men are lost along the way, and old adversaries return. But nothing can prepare them for the events that will unfold by the church of Cathures, on the shores of the great River Clud.

The fourth instalment of the Druid Stones Saga, tales of Celtic history and magic set in 9th century Scotland.

Available at your preferred store here **https://books2read.com/Dr uidStones3**

About the Author

J. F. Danskin is a Scottish writer of fantasy novels. His work spans several sub-genres and he is currently writing and publishing the *Druid Stones Saga*, a historical fantasy series and the LitRPG *Shadow Kingdoms* series.

Published titles by J. F. Danskin
    The Broken Circle (Book 1 of the Druid Stones Saga)
    The Twisted Forest (Book 2 of the Druid Stones Saga)
    The Mythic Spear (Book 3 of the Druid Stones Saga)
    The Winter Tower (Book 4 of the Druid Stones Saga)
    Shadow Kingdoms: The Knights of Dawn (Book 1 of the Shadow Kingdoms Series)
    Shadow Kingdoms: The Call of the Coven (Book 2 of the Shadow Kingdoms Series)

Forthcoming titles:
    The Wyvern Gate (Book 5 of the Druid Stones Saga)
    Shadow Kingdoms: Book 3 of the contemporary LitRPG series
    Sparta Online: Book 1 - a new historical LitRPG adventure

Connect with me:
    http://www.jfdanskin.com
    https://www.facebook.com/jfdanskin

https://bookhip.com/JKLSDR